FLAME

It was imperative that Rachel should go
off to Colombia to find her brother, who
was searching for a treasure of emeralds—
but her only chance of success lay with
Vitas de Mendoza. He agreed to help
her—but at a price. Would she find the
price too high? Or would she pay it—
far too willingly?

SOLITAIRE

Solitaire, her kindly Uncle Jim's house in the Vendée region of France, represented a welcoming haven after years of unhappiness—but Marty arrived there to find her uncle gone and in his place a hard, unwelcoming stranger—Luc Dumarais. There would be no haven at Solitaire now, she realised. And if she did not get away quickly, there would be even more unhappiness ... for Luc Dumarais was right out of her league ...

MOTH TO THE FLAME

To help her selfish sister Jan to marry Mario Vallone, against the wishes of his stern brother Santino, Juliet pretended to be Jan. And all she got for her pains was to be whisked off to a lonely part of Calabria, with a man who had the lowest possible opinion of her—and whose attraction she was finding it increasingly hard to resist ...

HIGH TIDE AT MIDNIGHT

When the only relatives she had in the world made it plain that she was unwelcome in their house, Morwenna took herself defiantly off to some old friends of her mother's in Cornwall, hoping they would offer her a home. She had gone there to ask a favour, but as things turned out she remained to bestow one—but at the expense of her peace of mind.

DRAGON'S LAIR

The marriage of Davina and Gethyn Lloyd had been brief and disastrous, and they had not met for two years. Now circumstances had thrown them together again—and Davina knew that her feelings for Gethyn, far from fading, were stronger than ever. But how could she ever sort out the tangle of misunderstanding that still lay between them?

FLAME OF DIABLO

BY

SARA CRAVEN

MILLS & BOON LIMITED
17–19 FOLEY STREET
LONDON W1A 1DR

First published 1979
Australian copyright 1979
Philippine copyright 1979
This edition 1979

© Sara Craven 1979

ISBN 0 263 73133 2

Set in Linotype Plantin 10 on 10½ pt.

Made and printed in Great Britain by
Richard Clay (The Chaucer Press), Ltd., Bungay, Suffolk

CHAPTER ONE

A FEW flakes of snow were drifting down from a leaden sky as Rachel Crichton paid off the taxi, and ran up the shallow flight of steps to the front door. Her urgent ring at the bell was answered almost immediately by a tall thin woman in a neat dark dress, a smile of thankfulness relieving the anxiety in her face.

'Oh, Miss Rachel, you've come at last! He's been asking and asking for you. Dr Kingston wants to move him to the Mordaunt Clinic, and he won't go. Said he had to see you first. He's been getting himself in a real state—and Miss Rachel, he mustn't!'

'I know.' Rachel gave the housekeeper's hand a comforting squeeze. Even after twenty years, Mrs Thurston still had not been able to come to terms with Sir Giles Crichton's arrogant refusal to allow any denial of his wishes. 'I came as soon as I got your message. How—how is he?' She made a little helpless gesture. 'This is the last thing I was expecting. He seemed to have got over the last attack . . .'

She paused, and saw Mrs Thurston give a little shake of her head.

'It's bad this time, Miss Rachel, the worst yet. That's why Doctor Kingston wants to move him. He told him to his face that he couldn't be trusted to rest properly here.' She swallowed. 'I was with him when it happened, and I thought we were going to lose him, that I did.'

'Oh, Thursty!' Rachel stared at her in dismay. 'It must have been awful for you. I should have been here—the play closed over a week ago.'

'It wouldn't have made much difference.' Mrs Thurston seemed to rouse herself from her anxiety, and moved to help Rachel off with her coat. 'Sir Giles has hardly been here himself for the past fortnight. He's been backwards

5

and forwards to London nearly every day. He even spent the night there one day last week. And when I tried to remind him of what the doctor had said, he nearly bit my head off. I said no more, naturally, but I'm wondering now whether, if I hadn't given up so easily, this might have been avoided.'

'I don't think so, Thursty darling. And you're not to blame yourself.' Rachel gave a soft sigh. 'We both know what Grandfather's like when he's got the bit between his teeth. But what can he have been doing in London? Did he give no hint?'

'None at all, Miss Rachel.' The older woman hesitated. 'But he seemed—different. More like his old self. I wondered if it might have something to do with Mr Mark.'

'I don't think so, Thursty,' Rachel said gently. 'But we can always hope. Now, I'd better go up.'

She ran up the broad, shallow flight of stairs which led to the first floor bedrooms, and turned along the landing to the big double doors of the room situated at the far end. As she approached they opened, and a slight grey-haired man emerged. He looked tired and anxious, but his eyes lit up when he saw her, and he laid a finger conspiratorially over his lips, glancing back towards the room he had left.

'Uncle Andrew?' she whispered. 'How is he?'

'No worse, but certainly no better either,' he said quietly. 'Your arrival should help. He's under sedation, and I rely on you, Rachel, not to allow him to get excited in any way. Now that you're here I'll go and arrange about that ambulance.' He patted her cheek and went on past her towards the stairs.

It was very warm in the bedroom. A fire had been kindled in the old-fashioned grate, and its leaping flames together with a shaded bedside lamp provided all the light in the room.

Her grandfather lay back against the pillows, his eyes closed. He was very pale, and there was a bluish tinge around his mouth which frightened her, but she was careful not to let the fright show as she trod across the carpet, her slender feet noiseless in their low-heeled shoes. There was a chair close beside the bed, and she sat down on it, waiting for him to open his eyes and notice her there, unwilling to disturb him purposely.

At last his eyes did open, still fiercely blue, but with some of their former fire dimmed. For a moment Sir Giles gazed at her almost without recognition, then his glance sharpened and focussed, and he said, 'So you're here at last.'

Rachel tried to ignore the implied reproach in his words of greeting, to forget that if he'd been backwards and forwards to London as Mrs Thurston had said, there had been plenty of opportunities for him to contact her if he'd wanted—opportunities that had remained neglected. She tried to forget too that the reproach had always been there, ever since, in fact, the longed-for first grandchild had been born a girl instead of the boy he had set his heart on, and had not been alleviated even with Mark's birth some two and a half years later.

She bent over the bed and put her lips to his cheek. 'I'm here, Grandfather. Can I get you a drink or anything?'

'No, child.' The effort of speaking seemed to be using up his breath at an alarming rate, she thought. 'Just—listen.'

He closed his eyes again and lay still, absorbed with some interior struggle for strength. She was just beginning to grow uneasy, when he said, 'Have you heard from Mark?'

'No, darling,' she said gently. 'Not a word.'

He gave a slight nod. 'Not important. I—know where he is.'

'You know?' Rachel felt a stab of anger. 'And you never told me? You never . . .'

'I'm telling you now, child,' he interrupted testily, and she subsided, remembering what the doctor had said about not letting him become excited. 'It was by chance I found out. I had to go up to Town to see old Grainger. I was having lunch at the club afterwards when Larry Forsyth walked in. Do you remember him?'

'I think so,' Rachel returned almost mechanically, her

brain still whirling from the news she had just received. 'Wasn't he in the diplomatic service?'

Her grandfather gave a grunt. 'Still is. He's been out in Colombia for a couple of years. And that's where he saw Mark, less than three weeks ago.'

'In Colombia?' Rachel shook her head. 'It sounds most unlikely. Was he sure it was Mark?'

'Of course he was sure!' Sir Giles sounded irritable. 'Knew him at once, and Mark recognised him too. He was dining with some people—name of Arviles. Señor Arviles is one of the top lawyers in Bogota, according to Larry.'

'Mark was at university with someone called Arviles— Miguel Arviles,' Rachel said slowly. 'But I didn't know he was a Colombian. And I didn't realise that Mark was on particularly close terms with him either.'

But then, she thought, why should she had known? Mark had never been forthcoming about his friendships, and Rachel had had to learn to curb her curiosity, knowing that any suspicion of over-protectiveness would be resented.

She frowned a little. 'Did Mr Forsyth know what Mark was actually doing there?'

'Of course not. He assumed I would know all about it and I allowed him to think so, or did you imagine I was prepared to make him cognisant of our private affairs?' Sir Giles' eyes glared a little under the bushy white brows and Rachel said hurriedly,

'No, no. It was silly of me. Did—did Mark send any kind of message?'

'Apparently he had very little to say for himself,' her grandfather said shortly. 'That's why I asked whether you'd heard from him. It occurred to me that as he must realise his whereabouts are now known, he might have been in touch.' He was silent for a moment, his breathing ragged.

Rachel was silent too, remembering. There had been family rows before, some of them quite spectacular, as when she had announced her intention of going to drama school, but somehow she had known they had not really been important. Grandfather had been irritated by the idea of her wishing to become an actress and had expressed his views forcibly, but she had always suspected he was merely going through the motions. It didn't really matter to him what Rachel did with her working life, because she would merely be filling in time before she made a suitable marriage.

But Mark was different. Grandfather had plans for Mark, and had never made any secret of the fact, and none of these plans took into account Mark's openly acknowledged passion for geology, and his desire to study it at university. Harsh words had been uttered on both sides, but Mark had got his way in the end—as he usually did, Rachel thought resignedly. Perhaps Grandfather had thought it was just a boyish quirk from which Mark would recover in his own good time if left unopposed. Only it hadn't been like that. When he had left university, it was to seek work as a geologist, not to succumb to the none too subtle pressure being exerted to make him join the family firm.

And that was when the real row had started. Rachel had been staying at Abbots Field during that weekend, and she had been powerless to intercede while her grandfather and her brother prepared to tear each other to pieces.

The trouble was they were too alike in many ways, she thought. Neither of them could easily see any point of view other than his own, or even believe that such a thing existed. The weekend had been full of tensions—rather like duellists, she had thought afterwards, selecting their weapons and taking the prescribed paces, but the first shots had not been exchanged until Sunday evening at dinner, just when she'd begun to hope that an open confrontation might be avoided. They'd quickly passed from veiled remarks to open recriminations, both of them becoming angrier and less accessible to reason with every moment that passed, with Rachel sitting in between them, a helpless spectator, trying to resist the urge to press her hands over her ears and shut out the cruel hurtful things they were hurling at each other.

'You'll be a pauper, boy, d'you hear me? A pauper!'

Sir Giles had crashed his fist down on the table making the silver and glasses jump. 'What can you expect but some minor post in a beggarly university department—spending your vacations taking elderly maiden ladies on fossil-hunting expeditions. What kind of life is that for a Crichton?'

'My God, you make me sick!' Mark had jumped to his feet, his face crimson with temper. 'You and your preconceived ideas of everyone outside your narrow bigoted experience! Why, you don't even know the kind of salary a top class geologist can command from an oil industry these days.'

'Top class—you?' Sir Giles had laughed sneeringly. 'It takes years, boy, to get to the top in any profession, and you didn't even get an Honours degree. You'll be back here in a year, moaning that you can't manage on your salary, begging me for a hand-out. Well, wait and see what answer you get!'

Mark was white where he had been red before. He leaned across the table, staring his grandfather in the face. His voice was very even and distinct as he said, 'If and when I ever do come back, I'll be rich. I'll have so much bloody money that I'll make you eat every word you've said. And I shan't come back until I've got it.'

He'd walked out of the room, and Rachel had gone after him, but it had been no use. He'd looked at her almost as if he didn't see her, and her pleadings had been to no avail.

In the end she'd said, 'Mark, he's an old man. You can't do this to him. You can't—just walk out like this.'

His remote look deepened. 'Does age give you the right to ride roughshod over everyone? We've had it all our lives, Rachie, ever since Mother and Father died, and I've had enough of it. He's had pre-ordained slots for both of us, and I'm not going to humour him any longer. He seems to think the only wealth in the world is to be found in the City of London. Well, I'm going to teach him that he's wrong.' His hand came up and touched her cheek. 'I'll be back one day, Rachie. Don't worry about me.'

It had been a week later that Grandfather had suffered

his first minor attack, and Rachel, panicking and sending for Mark, had discovered that he was nowhere to be found. He had given up his flat and apparently vanished into thin air. She did the rounds of his closest friends, but none of them knew, or professed not to know, where he had gone. And she'd waited, endlessly, for the phone call, the letter, the message of reassurance which did not come.

And now, six months later, Sir Giles had suffered yet another attack, and this time he was really ill. Every bone in the proud old face seemed suddenly prominent beneath the transparency of his skin, and Rachel felt a sudden dryness invade her mouth as she looked at him. Was he— could he be dying? Uncle Andrew had never suggested a nursing home before, especially a high-powered one like the Mordaunt Clinic. She sank her teeth into the softness of her lower lip and waited for the sick man to speak again.

He moved restlessly at last and opened his eyes again, blinking a little as if even the muted light in the room hurt them.

He said hoarsely, 'I was going to fetch him, Rachel. It's all in the desk downstairs—my air ticket, hotel reservation in Bogota—everything. I'd planned to leave next week as soon as the inoculations took effect. You'll have to go instead.'

For a dazed moment she thought her ears had deceived her—or that she was going mad.

Then she saw his eyes fixed on her with almost painful intensity, and heard him repeat, 'You'll have to go, Rachel. It's the only way. Bring the boy home to me— before it's too late.'

Andrew Kingston said angrily, 'It's the most ridiculous thing I've ever heard of. You can't seriously mean that you're going?'

Rachel said wearily, 'What choice do I have? You've told me yourself how ill he is—that another attack could occur at any time and be fatal. He wants to see Mark before he dies. It's understandable. He's his heir, after all.'

Dr Kingston moved his shoulders sceptically. They were in his private office at the Mordaunt Clinic, a tray of freshly made coffee on the desk between them. Sir Giles had been brought there by ambulance only half an hour before and was now in an intensive care unit. Rachel had been in to wish him goodnight, but he had been under heavy sedation and had not recognised her.

He said, 'My dear child——' and paused, apparently lost for words.

She smiled rather wearily. 'He has it all arranged. He even has an appointment tomorrow for all the various jabs—yellow fever, cholera—you name it. I'm supposed to keep the appointment in his place. The bookings are made, and my passport is in order. I don't need a visa as I don't expect to stay more than ninety days. It—couldn't be better.'

Dr Kingston's frown intensified. 'My dear, it couldn't be worse. What can Giles be thinking of? A beautiful young woman like you—alone in South America of all places!'

She said quietly, 'He's thinking of Mark.'

There was a brief unhappy silence while Andrew Kingston looked at her across the desk. There had been a feature article about her recently in one of the Sunday papers. It had described her jibingly as the 'Ice Maiden' of the English stage, and perhaps that was the impression she gave, with her cool blonde beauty and air of rather aloof composure. But a more discerning writer, he thought, might have detected the vulnerability beneath the poise which betrayed itself in the soft curves of her mouth, and the faint shadow which so often lurked in her green eyes.

He said abruptly, 'But what about your career? The play you're in—and that panel game on television?'

She smiled. 'The play closed—and I've finished my stint on that particular game. My agent has other offers which I've been considering, but there's nothing as yet that I feel I would die rather than miss. For all practical purposes

I could go to Colombia. I've been promising myself a holiday, and it would get me away from the English winter.'

'Oh, it would do that all right,' said Doctor Kingston
grimly.

Rachel leaned forward, setting down her empty cup. 'I
told him I'd go,' she said quietly.

'What?'

'You told me not to let him get excited. He saw that I
was hesitating and he started to get—very excited, so I
had to agree. He wants Mark home. It means everything
to him—the sorting out of this stupid quarrel. Mark won't
refuse to come back with me when he knows what the situation is.'

'But do you have to be the one to tell him?' he demanded. 'This fellow—Forsyth—who saw Mark in Bogota.
Couldn't he arrange something—have the boy traced?'

Rachel sighed. 'But don't you see that would mean including other people—strangers—in a family upset? Grandfather wouldn't be able to bear that. You're really the only
person outside the family who knows what happened, and
you're my godfather, so that makes it—legal, I suppose.
And it isn't really so onerous, you know. The arrangements
have all been made for me. All I have to do is fly out to
Bogota next week, trace this Arviles family and persuade
Mark to come home—that is if he wants to see Grandfather alive.' She swallowed painfully. 'I doubt if I'll be
in the country more than forty-eight hours.'

Doctor Kingston nodded almost absently, his fingers
playing with the cap of his fountain pen. Then he said
gently, 'My dear child, what are you trying to prove?'

He saw the colour rise in her face. 'That isn't fair!'

'It's the truth, Rachel, so what about it?'

She got up from her chair and went over to the window,
pulling back the curtain and looking out into the darkness. She said, 'Do you know, it's snowing quite hard
now.' And then with barely a change of tone, 'Don't you
see, Uncle Andrew, he's asked me to do this for him. It's
the first time in my life that he's ever asked me for something. He's always been the one to give—you know that,

ever since Mother and Father died. And he always made it clear that no return was ever expected or wanted, because I was a girl.'

'But he's always been proud of you. And you're making a name for yourself in the theatre now. That must please him.'

She smiled wryly and let the curtain fall back into place.

'Grandfather has always secretly believed that women belong in two places—and the theatre is neither of them. He has always looked on my career as a curious aberration which will be cured when I do the right thing and marry, and produce a family—boys, naturally.'

'Rachel!'

'Oh, it's true, Uncle Andrew, and we both know it. He forgave me for my sex a long time ago, but he's never let me forget it either—until now—and I'm not going to let slide an opportunity for Grandfather to see me as a person. I want him—I need him to be grateful to me, and if that sounds an unworthy motive for going to find Mark, then I'm sorry, but it's the only one I've got.'

She swung back towards him, her lips smiling and her eyes luminous with unshed tears.

She said lightly, 'I'm relying on you to give me the necessary shots, Uncle Andrew. I'd rather it was you than this strange doctor that Grandfather has found. You know what a coward I am.'

Andrew Kingston said soberly, 'That isn't quite the word I'd have used, my dear. But if your mind is made up, then I'll say no more.'

Rachel leaned her aching head against the cool glass of the cab window and stared out at the rain-washed streets that they were so rapidly traversing. It had been a long and tiring journey and she was beginning to wish that she had obeyed her first impulse and stretched out on the comfortable bed in her hotel room. As it was, she had stayed only long enough to register and leave her luggage before enquiring at the desk if they could provide her with Señor Arviles' address.

The *señor* seemed to be quite as well known as Larry Forsyth had said, for within a matter of minutes a taxi had been summoned by the helpful clerk, and Rachel was on her way to the expensive suburbs which lay to the north of Bogota beneath the towering and slightly oppressive peaks of the Andes.

It was much cooler than she had anticipated, and Rachel found she was glad of the cream-coloured suit in fine wool she was wearing. What little she knew about the prevailing climate in Latin America did not seem to apply to Bogota, and she supposed vaguely that this was due at least in part to the fact that the city lay at over eight thousand feet above sea level.

She'd intended to do some background reading before setting out, but the days had slipped past with increasing acceleration, and the day of her departure was upon her almost before she knew it. Apart from packing, and spending an uncomfortable day reacting from her injections, she'd visited her grandfather daily.

On her last visit, she'd received the cheering news that he seemed to be out of immediate danger, and wasn't altogether surprised as she entered his room to hear that he'd undergone a change of heart about her trip.

Sir Giles was all set to make plans to visit Colombia himself as soon as he was back on his feet again, and it required a stern visit from Andrew Kingston, spelling out to him precisely how long that might take, to reconcile him to the fact that Rachel was going in his place.

Instead he contented himself with uttering dire warnings about the kinds of attitude that Rachel might encounter on her trip.

'They're an old-fashioned society out there still.' He fixed Rachel with a glare. 'None of your Women's Lib nonsense. Women have their place and they keep to it.'

'Haven't I always?' Rachel asked with a trace of bitter humour in her voice.

Sir Giles' glance was still fierce, but there was a tinge of discomfort in it. 'You're a good child,' he admitted almost unwillingly. 'But you're a good-looking one too, and you'll be mixing with men with the blood of the *conquistadores* in their veins. Have you thought about that?'

Rachel lifted an arched eyebrow. 'I always thought they were more interested in gold than in personal conquests,' she said. 'And I'm perfectly able to take care of myself, you know. I've been working in the theatre—remember?— and they call me the Ice Maiden.'

'Lot of damned nonsense,' Sir Giles rumbled. 'And written by that fellow who was supposed to be keen on you. What happened? Did you quarrel?'

Rachel was silent for a moment. One could not tell one's devoted and old-fashioned grandfather the truth— that Leigh's article had been prompted by nothing more than sexual pique, because he'd suddenly discovered he was not as irresistible as he'd always thought.

She'd liked Leigh, and frankly enjoyed the kudos of being seen with one of Fleet Street's youngest and most attractive show business columnists. And eventually, inevitably there had started to be more to it than that. He'd become more than attractive. He'd begun to be necessary to her. Afterwards when she could think about it clearly and rationally, she could see what he had done—how clever he had been. He'd always known she wouldn't be a pushover like most of his girl-friends, so he'd played the game her way, making his approach a gentle, almost insidious one, even making her believe, God help her, that he was falling in love with her.

She had even invited him down to Abbots Field for the weekend, although it had not been a great success, as she was the first to admit. Leigh's elegant boutique-bought clothes and slightly raffish charm had seemed out of place against the quiet gracious lines of the old house, and although Sir Giles had behaved with perfect correctness, Rachel knew all the same that he was not impressed with Leigh. It had been a disappointment, but not, she had told herself optimistically, an insurmountable one. Grandfather and Leigh had to be given a chance to come to terms, occupying as they did, two very different worlds.

But there had been no opportunity for that. The following weekend Leigh had invited her to go away with him, to meet his family, he'd said. She'd accepted gladly, but then the doubts had begun. His manner had changed subtly, for one thing, and then for someone travelling home for the weekend he didn't seem altogether sure of the route. And when they arrived at the secluded cottage, and found it deserted, she knew, and dismissed all Leigh's too-fluent excuses about mistaken dates. The cottage wasn't his home. He'd simply hired it for the weekend. He'd admitted as much eventually, amused at her dismay, but clearly confident of his ability to win her over and persuade her to stay there with him as his mistress.

'But I don't want it to be like this,' she'd cried at last. 'It's dirty—it's sordid—and if you loved me, you wouldn't want it like this either.'

The memory of his laughter still had the power to make her cringe as if something slimy had left a trail across her skin. That, and the things he had said to her which had killed any feelings she'd had for him—the first sweet stirrings of desire that he'd roused in her—stone dead.

The Ice Maiden article had appeared two weeks later under his byline. It was skilful, even humorous, but Rachel recognised as she'd been meant to do the sting in the tail, and knew that, at a time when female sexuality was being exploited in the theatre, she was being written of as shallow, naïve and frigid. Everyone knew of her relationship with Leigh, and would assume that he knew what he was talking about.

Only his spite had misfired. A role in a television play that she'd not expected to get was suddenly offered to her, and for the first time in her career she was almost overwhelmed with work. Her agent, who had groaned over the Ice Maiden article, was surprised and delighted, and her success had helped in some way to relieve the ache Leigh's treachery had caused her.

'Yes,' she said quietly at last, aroused from her painful reverie by the knowledge that her grandfather was becoming restive, 'you could say that we—quarrelled.'

Sir Giles grunted. 'Well, he's no great loss to you, my

dear. I can't say I took to him. Strange sense of values he seems to have.'

She nodded silently, a feeling of desolation striking at her.

In the weeks which followed she had lived up to the image that Leigh had bestowed upon her, holding aloof from all emotional attachments, pretending that she preferred her own company, learning to conceal the harsh facts of her own loneliness. At least, she had tried to console herself, she had Grandfather and Mark to rely on. But then had come that terrible night at Abbots Frields, and it seemed as if Mark too had deserted her.

Rachel gave herself an impatient little shake and sat up, studying her surroundings. The streets the taxi was passing through seemed to combine a multitude of styles with glass skyscrapers springing up next to buildings of the old Spanish colonial tradition, and the elaborate façades of public buildings and churches. It could be an intriguing place, she decided, perched high on its Andean plateau and it was a pity that she had not more time at her disposal to explore. Perhaps after she'd made contact with Mark and persuaded him to return to England with her, there might be a brief opportunity then, she thought hopefully.

The scenery was changing as they left the more commercial districts behind and entered the purely residential area. There was no sign here of any poverty or decay in these gracious mansions with their velvet lawns and fountain-bedecked gardens. It all spoke of peace and tranquillity and the solid comfort that money can bring. And the Arviles family were part of all this, she realised, as the taxi turned into one of the smooth curving drives.

It was a charming house, low and rambling, a fragrant creeper burgeoning with pale pink blossoms cascading down to the ground beside the front door as Rachel knocked. She had told the taxi to wait for her. If Mark was there, she told herself hopefully, he might pack and come with her straight away. They could drive to the airport and pick up the next flight out.

When the door opened she was confronted by a stout

woman in a dark dress covered by a white apron, who regarded Rachel with a doubtful frown. Relying on the Spanish phrase book she had bought at the airport, Rachel asked if she might speak to Señor Arviles. For a moment she was afraid that she had not made herself understood, for the woman frowned a little as if puzzled, but she held the door open for Rachel to enter.

The entrance hall was large with a coolly tiled floor. Rachel followed the maid to a large *salón* at the back of the house, where it was intimated she should wait. It was beautifully furnished and the chairs looked comfortable as well as luxurious, but Rachel felt too restless to sit down and compose herself. Her headache was worse too, and she felt an odd dizziness.

I'm a fool, she thought. I should have rested and had something to eat before I came here. But the thought of food, hungry though she was, was suddenly and grossly unappealing, and she was thankful when the door behind her opened, diverting her mind from her own physical discomfort.

A small, rather plump woman came in, followed by a young girl. The physical resemblance between them was too pronounced for them to be anything but mother and daughter, but where the girl was dressed with a demure and expensive simplicity, the older woman had a stunning and moneyed elegance. She wore black, and there was a discreet glitter of diamonds on her hands and at her throat, and she smiled rather uncertainly at Rachel.

The girl stepped forward. 'You asked for my father,' she said in heavily accented English. 'I regret that he is not here. My mother wishes to be of assistance, but she speaks no English. How can we help you, *señorita*?'

'My name is Rachel Crichton.' Rachel paused. 'I was hoping that my brother might be here—or that you might know where he was?'

She had to wait while the girl translated what she had said for the *señora*, and then Señora Arviles came forward with both hands outstretched. Rachel only understood about one word in ten of what she was saying, but she knew she was being made welcome, and she smiled in response.

The girl came forward too, her lips curving piquantly. 'So you are the sister of Marcos. I am Isabel. He has mentioned me, perhaps.'

'He hasn't mentioned anyone,' Rachel returned rather awkwardly. 'I—we've rather lost touch over the past month or two, I'm afraid. That's why I'm here. Our grandfather is very ill, and he wants to see Mark.'

Isabel looked bewildered. She spread her hands prettily. 'But he is not here, *señorita*. He has not been here since three weeks. We understood he was returning to Gran Bretaña. Is this not so?'

Rachel's heart sank within her. She had come all this way for nothing. For all she knew Mark might be back in England at this moment. He might even have gone to Abbots Field.

'You are pale, *señorita*.' Isabel urged her to sit down, and she was glad to because her legs felt like jelly.

'But he was staying with you,' she persisted.

'*Si*. He was with Miguel. He likes to bring friends here to stay.'

'Perhaps Miguel would know exactly where he was,' Rachel said half to herself. 'Could—could I have a word with him?'

Isabel's eyes widened. 'He is not here, *señorita*. He has gone to Cartagena to stay with the family of his *novia*.'

The *señora* broke in, clearly intrigued by the exchange between the two girls and wanting to know its subject. While Isabel explained to her mother, Rachel sat her head whirling. She didn't know what to do next. She supposed she ought to try and make contact with the Mordaunt Clinic to see if Mark had turned up there. She pressed a hand against her throbbing head, willing herself to think straight. Perhaps there was some way she could enquire if Mark had left the country. She would have to arrange to see Señor Arviles. He was a lawyer, after all. He would be able to advise her.

She looked up, and that was a mistake because the room

swam around her, and she could see Señora Arviles rising, her face full of concern.

'*Ay de mi*!' Isabel was at her side. 'What is the matter, *señorita*?'

Rachel said through dry lips, 'I'm afraid I'm going to be sick.'

The next few hours in retrospect were like a nightmare. She knew that somehow they had got her out of the *salón* and upstairs to a bedroom. Then someone was there called Dolores, helping to remove the cream suit with warm capable hands, holding a basin while Rachel vomited until her stomach was sore and bathing her forehead with a cool damp cloth in between spasms.

Rachel wanted to tell her that she was grateful, but she was too dizzy and too weak, and every attempt to raise her head from the pillow seemed to bring on another attack of nausea. She wasn't even aware that at last she had drifted into an exhausted sleep.

When she opened her eyes, the room was dark except for one heavily shaded lamp in the corner. She stirred and stretched cautiously, but her body seemed to respond normally to the action, and she risked sitting up. As she did so, the door opened cautiously and Isabel's head came round it.

'Ah, you are awake,' she exclaimed. 'That is good. Do you feel better now? Well enough to speak to my father?'

Rachel nodded, thankful that there was no return of that appalling dizziness as she did so. 'I'm sorry to have put you to so much trouble,' she said contritely.

'What trouble?' Isabel shrugged. 'It is the altitude which makes one suffer in this way. Many *turistas* are afflicted when they first arrive here, but one soon becomes acclimatised.'

She produced a large silk shawl which she proceeded to drape carefully round Rachel's bare shoulders, then sending her a flashing smile she went back to the door and admitted her father.

Señor Arviles was a dapper man of medium height with an intelligent, humorous face. He bowed slightly over

Rachel's hand, then drew up a chair and sat down beside her bed. Rachel was amused to see that Isabel remained in the room, presumably to act as a youthful chaperone.

After an exchange of civilities, he came swiftly to the point.

'I am grieved that we can give you no news of your brother, *señorita*. But we all understood that he was to return home to England. Has he not done so?'

Rachel shook her head. 'Apparently not. And I need to contact him urgently, *señor*.'

'So Isabel has told me. A family illness, is it not?' Señor Arviles gave her a sympathetic look. 'Believe me, I would help if it were possible, but your brother merely stayed with us for a short while, then went on his way. His visit was shorter than we would have liked,' he added courteously, 'because he knew Miguel was to go to Cartagena.'

'I see.' Rachel paused. 'He didn't give the impression that he intended to stay in Colombia, maybe?'

'No, *señorita*.' Señor Arviles shook his head. 'While he stayed with us, Miguel and he made tours, and paid visits to places of interest. There would be little left for him to see, I think.'

'No,' Rachel said desolately. 'I suppose he must have— moved on somewhere.'

She would have to go home and confess failure, she thought unhappily, and what would that do to Grandfather's already precarious health? She could only be glad that it was she who had had the wasted journey to the other side of the world, and not Sir Giles.

Señor Arviles' eyes studied her downbent head attentively.

He said, 'In the meantime, *señorita,* you will spend a few days with us? We are happy to welcome the sister of Marcos to our house.'

'Oh, but I couldn't.' Rachel shook her head. 'I've caused quite enough disruption already. Besides ...' She broke off, stricken, suddenly remembering. 'My God, I had a taxi waiting and...'

Señor Arviles laughed. 'It was paid off a long time ago, *señorita*, and the driver told us the name of your hotel so that we could contact them also. They might have become anxious if one so young and lovely had gone out into Bogota and not returned.'

Rachel returned his smile rather wanly. 'That's hardly likely.'

'You think not?' Señor Arviles shrugged. 'Yet you must remember, *señorita*, that this is Colombia, not Gran Bretaña. Our history has blood in it, and some of it is recent. You would do well to remain here with us, I think, and allow my wife and daughter to entertain you while I make what enquiries I can about Marcos.'

His tone was firm. It was the one he would use, Rachel decided, when he was giving a client some unpopular advice.

'So it is decided, then.' He rose briskly from the chair before she could utter a further protest. 'Rest, *señorita*, and we will make all necessary arrangements. Presently Dolores will bring you some soup.'

He bowed again and walked to the door. Isabel following him, her pretty face wearing a curiously thoughtful expression.

The soup when it came was delicious, almost a meal in itself, thick with beans and spiced meat, and served with delicately flavoured corn muffins.

Recalling how ill she had been only a short time before, Rachel was amazed that she could eat anything, but she finished every mouthful. When she heard the knock on the door, she imagined it was Dolores coming to remove her tray, and was surprised when Isabel came in.

She exclaimed with pleased politeness about Rachel's return to health, and sat down in the chair that her father had vacated, folding her hands in her lap. Watching her, Rachel thought suddenly that she looked troubled, and saw that her fingers gripped each other, tight with tension.

'There's something wrong, isn't there?' she said, cutting across Isabel's somewhat dutiful recital of the museums they would visit and the sights they would see while she remained in Bogota.

Isabel's eyes filled with sudden tears. 'Perhaps, *señorita*. I—I do not know.'

'Well, tell me what it is,' Rachel urged.

'But first you must promise that you must not tell my father.' Isabel's tone was equally urgent. 'He would be so angry—because I tell you and not him.'

'I promise I won't mention anything to him about this conversation.' Rachel's eyes never left the younger girl's face. 'Do you know where my brother has gone?'

Isabel lifted her shoulders in a deep shrug. 'Maybe— that is all I can say. *Señorita*, I must tell you something now of which I am much ashamed.' She paused. 'I love my brother, but sometimes he is not kind. Sometimes, when he has his friends, he tells me to go away, to leave them in peace, and this hurts me. So they go to his room and they talk, and sometimes I go to my room where there is an *amario* on the wall next to Miguel's where there is also an *amario*.' She paused again. 'You know what I am trying to say?'

'I think so,' said Rachel. 'There are adjoining—wardrobes, perhaps, and you can—hear what they are talking about.'

Isabel blushed unhappily '*Si*, it is so. I am much ashamed now, but before I used to laugh to myself because Miguel thought he had his friends to himself, and I could not share in the things they talked about.'

Her eyes gleamed for a moment and Rachel thought that the sheltered daughter of the house had probably found her eavesdropping on purely masculine conversations more than enlightening at times.

She said, 'So you listened and you heard Mark and Miguel talking. Is that it?'

Isabel nodded. 'It was then I knew my father would be angry because Miguel had spoken to Marcos of forbidden things.'

'What forbidden things?'

Isabel looked down at her lap again. 'Emeralds,' she

said in a low voice. There was a long taut silence, then she went on. 'Our emerald mines here in Colombia, Señorita Raquel, are the most famous in the world. They make much money for our country. But not all the emeralds that leave Columbia do so with the will of our government, you understand.'

There was another pause and Rachel made herself say dry-mouthed, 'Smuggling? You mean Miguel and Mark were talking about smuggling emeralds?'

'Si, and from what Miguel is saying I know that he has done this thing, and that if my father ever finds out he will be angry, because it is so much against the law, and the law means everything to my father. He would think that Miguel had dishonoured him.'

Rachel said in a hollow voice, 'Do you mean that Miguel was suggesting that Mark should become an emerald smuggler?'

'No, not that. He seemed to be warning him. Many people die all the time because of emeralds. There is much danger. He says that he thinks your brother is a little mad. And then Señor Marcos says "You would not think I was so mad if I came back with the Flame of Diablo." '

'What is the Flame of Diablo?'

'It is a legend, Señorita Raquel, a story that I heard when I was a child, as did Miguel. It is said that somewhere in the hills to the north there is a mine where one can find emeralds worth many millions of *pesos*. But it is also said that no one has set eyes upon this mine since the days of El Dorado, the Golden One who used emeralds from the Diablo mine to ornament himself before he made the offering in the Sacred Lake.'

'Then Diablo is a place?' Rachel queried.

Isabel shuddered. 'It is truly named,' she said in a low voice, 'for it is a place of the devil. Many people seek the Diablo mine and the green flame which burns there, but they do not return. My father says the reason is simple. It is a dangerous place. Often there are landslides, and the rivers are deep with fierce currents and little fish that can eat a horse and rider before a man can utter a last prayer, and leave only the bones. And there is *el tigre* who kills, and many snakes. Also *bandidos* and other evil men,' she added, crossing herself. 'Perhaps it is all so, but there are those who say the reason why the Flame of Diablo stays hidden is that it is guarded by the old gods who were worshipped before the *conquistadores* came to this place, and that all who seek the Flame are accursed.'

In spite of herself, Rachel felt a long cold shiver run the length of her spine. It was all very well to tell herself robustly that only the very credulous would believe such a tale, but here in this alien land, in the very shadow of the pagan mountains, it was difficult to dismiss Isabel's recital as nonsense.

'And you think Mark has gone to this dreadful place?' she asked, steadying her voice.

Isabel's eyes met hers frankly. 'I did not, because Miguel talks much to your brother, telling him of the dangers. But now you come and tell us that he has not returned to Gran Bretaña, and I worry, because he told Miguel that was what he planned to do. I think perhaps he only told Miguel this to put his mind at ease, so that he would not blame himself for having told him the legend. There are many such stories, you understand. I think Miguel did not believe Marcos would take him seriously.'

'Mark's a geologist,' Rachel said, passing her tongue over her dry lips. 'I suppose he might think that if this mine existed he had as good a chance as any of finding it.' Or of dying, her mind ran crazily on. Of being drowned in a river, or eaten by piranha fish, or shot by bandits, or even swept off a mountain ledge by a giant condor. Hadn't she read somewhere that they sometimes attacked unwary travellers?

Isabel's cold little hand crept into hers. Her great dark eyes looked enormous suddenly, too large for her pinched face.

'What will you do, *señorita*?'

'I don't know,' Rachel said rather helplessly. 'After all, we have no real proof that that's where Mark has gone, although it does seem more than likely.'

'If and when I ever do come back, I'll be rich. I'll have so much bloody money, I'll make you eat every word you've said. And I shan't come back until I've got it.'

The words seemed to sting and burn in her brain. Through Miguel Arviles, Mark now knew of the possible existence of an emerald mine which could fulfil his wild promise. Also through Miguel he could know of a way to get any gems that he found out of the country. Generations ago there had been a wild streak in the Crichtons. Perhaps this streak had been reborn in Mark, blinding him to all aspects of the perilous game he was playing but its high stakes.

Rachel smiled reassuringly into Isabel's anxious eyes.

'I expect I shall go back to England myself,' she said untruthfully. 'After all, we may be making mountains out of molehills.'

'Que quiere decir eso?' Isabel's brow wrinkled. 'What is this molehill?'

'It doesn't matter,' Rachel assured her. 'I—I'll inform the authorities here that Mark—seems to be missing, so that they can keep an eye open for him, but there isn't much more I can do.'

'No,' Isabel agreed, but so despondently that Rachel was tempted to throw caution to the winds and tell her that she intended to set out for Diablo herself the following day. But she restrained herself. Isabel might fear her father's wrath, but Rachel felt sure that would not prevent her telling Señor Arviles about her plans if she got wind of them, and he, Rachel did not doubt, would take steps to prevent her from doing anything so foolhardy.

She soothed her conscience by telling herself she did not want to cause the Arviles family any more anxiety on her behalf. But she knew in her heart that this was not altogether true. Perhaps it was not only in Mark that the forgotten wild streak had surfaced.

I'm going to Diablo, she told herself, even if it means coming face to face with the devil himself.

CHAPTER TWO

THE bus rounded the bend with a lurch that almost had Rachel flying out of her seat. She controlled the startled cry which had risen to her lips, and settled herself more firmly. The other passengers seemed used to coping with the bus's vagaries, she noticed. Across the aisle, an Indian woman continued to feed her baby in the shelter of her *ruana,* her coppery face impassive. Rachel had seen as she boarded the bus that a small gaudy statue of the Virgin was secured just above the driver's seat, and there was a general tendency as the rickety vehicle rocked round a particularly hairpin bend, or swayed dangerously near the lip of some ravine, for the passengers and the driver to cross themselves devoutly.

Rachel could sympathise with this evidence of devotion, but she couldn't help wishing at the same time that the driver would keep both hands on the wheel.

She could understand now why the hotel clerk had stared at her in horror when she had enquired about buses, and strongly advised her to hire a car instead. Apart from her concern about the cost, she had not been keen to accept his advice. From what little she had seen of the drivers in Bogota, most of them seemed to regard a car as a symbol of their *machismo* and behave accordingly, Rachel possessed a driving licence, but she doubted her ability to compete, and now that she had seen the standard of the road up to Asuncion, she was glad she had not tried. She tried to imagine meeting one of these buses on one of those bends, and shuddered inwardly.

The window she was sitting beside was covered in dust, but she couldn't really be sorry. At least she was being saved those stomach-turning glimpses of some of the valleys they had passed—a sheer rocky drop down to a wrinkled snake of a river. And snakes were another feature of the journey that she did not want to contemplate.

This whole trip was madness. She knew that now. What the hell did she think she was doing charging up a mountainside in company with a religious maniac masquerading as a bus driver, several crates of chickens and a goat?

She had seen the look of horrified disbelief come into the hotel clerk's eyes when she had asked him which was the nearest town to Diablo, and the most direct means of getting there. He had done his level best to dissuade her, protesting that such places were not for the *señorita*. Then he had tried to persuade her to hire a car, but had made the basic mistake of pointing out that at least then she would be under the protection of the driver. Something in the way he had said this had needled Rachel unbearably.

She had said clearly and coldly, 'I can look after myself, thank you, *señor*.'

It had been a briefly satisfying moment, but he still thought she was mad. She had seen it in his face as he turned away to deal with another guest. And now she tended to agree with him. She had never sat on a more uncomfortable seat, and she doubted whether the bus itself had any springs. If she survived the journey, it would probably be as a hopeless cripple, she decided, as the base of her spine took another hammering.

It had been easier than she expected to persuade the Arviles family that she intended to return to England immediately, in pursuit of the errant Mark. Isabel had been disappointed that she would not even spend a couple of days with them, and Rachel regretted the necessity of deceiving the girl. But she wondered secretly if the *Señor* and the *Señora* might not have been quietly relieved at her departure, or could they genuinely have wanted yet another English visitor upsetting the smooth tenor of their life? Certainly she could not have faulted their hospitality.

She had tied a coloured handkerchief over her shoulder-length honey-coloured hair, and donned an enormous pair of sunglasses, but even so she knew that her fair hair and skin were attracting more attention than she desired from the mainly *mestizo* and Indian passengers, and she guessed

that few tourists must travel by this route—particularly
blonde, female English tourists.

She wondered if Mark had taken the same frankly death-
defying route before her, and had tried to put a few halting
questions to the driver before they had set off, but he had
stared at her uncomprehendingly, so she had given it up as
a bad job.

The bus seemed to be descending again, and slowly as
well. Peering down the bus, Rachel could detect a huddle
of buildings ahead of them, and guessed they had reached
Asuncion.

At first it seemed to bear a depressing resemblance to
other small settlements they had passed along the way, with
groups of tumbledown shacks lining a small rutted high-
way, but with a triumphant blast of its horn the bus wound
along the road, avoiding groups of children and animals
apparently attracted from the shack doorways to watch its
passing, and turned into a large square. Here some attempt
at least had been made to paint and generally refurbish the
buildings and there was a small market in progress. Presumably this was the final destination of the chickens and
the goat, Rachel decided, watching their descent from the
bus without a sense of overwhelming regret. They had
not been the quietest or the sweetest-smelling of travelling
companions.

As she alighted in her turn, she found the bus had
stopped outside a building which seemed to be Asuncion's
sole hotel. She glanced up at its peeling façade rather doubtfully. It wouldn't have been her first choice as an over-
night stop, but beggars could not be choosers, and besides,
there was an outside chance that Mark might have stayed
there.

The reception desk was deserted when she got there.
Rachel set down her small suitcase and looked around,
then rapped impatiently on the desk with her knuckles.
Almost as if her action had been a secret signal, a roar
of masculine laughter broke out quite close at hand. Rachel
jumped, then relaxed, moving her aching shoulders experimentally.

'I wish I could share the joke,' she muttered crossly.

Just then a door down the passage from the desk opened, and a man emerged. He paused before closing the door behind him and tossed a clearly jovial remark in Spanish over his shoulder, which was greeted with yet another burst of laughter. Then he spotted Rachel standing at the desk and his face changed in a moment, becoming both surprised and solemn.

'*Señorita*?' His tone as he approached was civil, but Rachel felt she was being very thoroughly assessed, and that there was a strong element of disapproval in his assessment.

She produced her phrase book, and began to laboriously recite a request for a room, but he waved the book aside.

'I speak a little English. You are an *inglesa, señorita*?'

'Yes, I am.' Relieved that she did not have to converse with him in her non-existent Spanish, Rachel smiled. 'I'm trying to trace another *inglese, señor*—a man. My brother,' she added hastily for some reason she probably could not have defined.

'He has been to Asuncion, this brother?' The man watched her impassively.

Rachel sighed. 'I'm not sure. I think so.'

He hesitated, then he reached for the hotel register and swung it round so that she could see it.

'Look for yourself, *señorita*. No *inglese* has been here apart from yourself.'

Rachel scanned swiftly down the list of names. It had occurred to her that Mark might have travelled under an assumed name, but she knew he would not have bothered to disguise his handwriting and none of the scrawls in the register bore the least resemblance to his signature. She felt almost sick with disappointment.

'*Turistas* do not come here, *señorita*,' the man said almost placidly. He was turning away, when she halted him.

'Then can I book a room for the night?' she asked, braving his look of astonishment. 'And a guide. I would like to hire a guide if that is possible.'

'*Señorita*,' the man said very slowly, 'I must tell you

that I do not have unescorted women staying at my hotel.'

She felt a slow tide of colour run up to the roots of her hair. She had never felt so helpless in her life.

She said, trying to keep her voice calm and pleasant, 'Then as this is the only hotel in this benighted town, I'm afraid you will have to make an exception for once. Unless you can provide me with a guide immediately, of course.'

His look of astonishment deepened. 'And where do you wish this guide to take you, *señorita*? Always supposing that such a person could be found.'

She said baldly, 'I want to go to Diablo.'

If she'd suddenly produced a hand grenade and drawn the pin, she couldn't have hoped to make a greater sensation. His jaw dropped, and he almost took a step backwards, she would have sworn to it.

He said flatly, '*Es imposible*. Where is your family, *señorita*? Who are your friends that they let you contemplate such madness?'

Rachel frowned. All sense of reality seemed to be slipping away from her, but that again could be attributed to the strangeness of the altitude. On the other hand it meant that she had to act the part she had set herself, and it was somehow easier to act than to believe in what she was doing. Deep down inside her she was afraid, but on the surface she was ice cool and in command of the situation.

She said, 'It's good of you to be so concerned, *señor*, but quite unnecessary. I can look after myself. I'm neither a child nor a fool, and I don't need you to judge my actions.'

Not a long speech, she thought detachedly, but an effective one, she hoped. In a situation like this, she needed to make every word count.

She glanced at the hotel-keeper, noting with satisfaction that he did not seem quite so sure of himself as he had been. There was an air of uncertainty about him, and he eyed her as if she was something new in his experience. She wanted to giggle, but that would be fatal, so she deepened her expression of calm assurance.

'There must be someone around here,' she said crisply.

'Someone who knows this region well. And you don't have to feel responsible for anything. Just introduce me to him, and I'll do the rest.'

The man gave her a long look, then shrugged deeply and fatalistically.

He said slowly, 'There is such a one—Vitas de Mendoza—but whether he will agree to take you to Diablo is another matter.'

'That's my problem,' she said confidently, almost gaily. She had talked round this definitely hostile little man. She could talk round the world. 'When can I meet him?'

He hesitated. 'Later, señorita. I will speak to him of your request. At the moment he is engaged.'

She saw him give a half-glance over his shoulder at that door down the passage, and remembered the sound of men's voices and laughter.

'I'd prefer to see him right away. The matter is urgent. I'm not just a casual sightseer, I'm looking for my brother.'

'And you think the brother has gone to Diablo.' He shook his head. 'That is not good, señorita, but it gives me an idea. Tomorrow or the next day there will be an army patrol arriving here. If you speak to Captain Lopez he will look for your brother.'

Rachel was silent for a moment. It was a tempting prospect to resign the responsibility for finding Mark to the army, but at the back of her mind she was remembering what Isabel had told her about the illegal trafficking in emeralds. Supposing when this Captain Lopez found Mark, he actually had emeralds in his possession? She swallowed. It didn't really bear thinking about. She had no idea of the sort of sentences attempts to smuggle emeralds might carry, but she imagined they would be heavy, and that Colombian prisons would be a bad scene too. Besides, if Mark were arrested, it would be the death of her grandfather.

She had to face the fact that she must find Mark herself—with the help of Vitas de Mendoza, and hope that he was the sort of man who could be bribed to keep his mouth shut if Mark had broken the law in any way. The thought

made her feel sick with fright and despair, but it also had
to be faced.

'I haven't got time to wait for the army,' she said. 'You
don't even know yourself when they'll be arriving, and they
could be held up. I've got to see this Mendoza man immediately. There'll be arrangements to make, and I want
to leave as soon as possible.'

She left her small case standing by the desk and went
down the passage towards the closed door. She wouldn't
have been at all surprised if he'd grabbed her arm and tried
to stop her as she passed him. When she reached the door
she risked a glance back over her shoulder, and saw that
he was standing quite still staring after her with an almost
bemused expression on his face, and she could have laughed
out loud.

All she had to do now was bemuse Vitas de Mendoza into
taking her to Diablo, she thought as she opened the door
and stepped into the room beyond.

It was a good job that she was still acting—making an
entrance—or what faced her when she entered the room
might have thrown her, like an unexpected laugh at a
serious moment in a play.

The air was so thick with cigar smoke that she could
hardly see across the room for the first moment or two,
and the acrid fumes caught at her throat. There were six
of them altogether, all men sitting round a table covered
in a green cloth. There were bottles and glasses, cards and
a scatter of money, and she felt bitterness rise in her throat
as she surveyed them. So this was the pressing engagement
which the hotel-keeper did not want to disturb.

Her gaze flickered round the table. She could read amaze-
ment on their faces, and the beginnings of a lewd appreciation in some of their smiles. And on one face—contempt.
Her eyes registered this and passed on, and almost in spite
of herself, looked back as though she had not believed what
she saw the first time.

He was younger than his companions—the mid-thirties
at the very most—dark as they all were, with raven black
hair springing back from a peak on his forehead. A thin

face, as fierce and arrogant as a hawk's, its harshness shockingly emphasised by the black patch he wore where his left eye should have been.

The man nearest the door pushed back his chair and stood up, smiling ingratiatingly at her. 'Come in, *chica*. You want to take a hand with us?' He spoke with a strong North America accent. The man next to him said something in Spanish, and a ribald roar of laughter went round the table.

But the man with the eye-patch didn't join in the general amusement. Rachel found her eyes being drawn unwillingly back to him yet again. He was dressed from head to foot in black, his shirt unbuttoned to halfway down his muscular chest. He leaned back in his chair, one booted leg swinging carelessly over its low wooden arm, but it seemed to Rachel that he was about as relaxed as a curled spring, or a snake rearing back to strike.

Isabel's voice sounded in her brain: '*Bandidos* and other evil men.'

The others seemed harmless enough—lecherous, perhaps, but harmless, but the man with the eye-patch was a very different proposition. She could believe that he was a bandit. She could see him in black velvet centuries before, a bloodstained sword in his hand as he cut down the defenceless Indians who stood between him and his dream of El Dorado. She could see him on the deck of some pirate ship, his face bleak and saturnine under that eye-patch as his ship's cannon raked the forts at Cartagena and Maracaibo.

And she could see him on the other side of this table looking at her as if she was dirt.

'Have a drink, *chica*.' The man who had got to his feet was leering at her, pushing a tumbler into her hand. The spirit it contained smelled sharp and raw, and her nose wrinkled in distaste, but she smiled politely as she refused. After all, he might turn out to be this Vitas de Mendoza, and she didn't want to offend him.

She smiled again, but this time there was a tinge of frost with it, setting them all at a distance. All except the man opposite, of course, who had already distanced himself, and him she would just have to ignore. She wondered what he was doing here. The others were obviously local businessmen enjoying the relaxation of a weekly card game. But who was he? A professional gambler, perhaps, if they had such things in Colombia. Certainly he seemed to have a larger pile of money lying in front of him than any of the others—ill-gotten gains, she thought, and caught at herself. This was ridiculous. She was standing here being fanciful and wasting precious time.

She said quietly but making sure her voice carried, 'I'm here to see Vitas de Mendoza, and I'd like to speak to him privately.'

She waited for one of the bronzed perspiring men around the table to step forward and identify himself, but no one moved, and a cold sick feeling of apprehension began to swell and grow inside her.

She said, 'He is here, isn't he?' and her voice shook a little because she knew already what the answer was, and she wished herself a million miles away.

The man nearest to her said quite jovially, 'Would I not do instead, *señorita*? *Dios*, Vitas, you have all the luck—with the cards and with the women!'

She looked past him to the man with the eye-patch and saw his lips twist, as if this was one piece of luck he would have preferred to do without. He made no attempt to alter his languid pose, merely leaning back further in his chair and staring at her with a frank, almost sensual appraisal which she found offensive in the extreme.

That hotel-keeper, she thought furiously, must be off his head if he imagined she was going to go off into the wide blue yonder with a man who looked as if his career had spanned the gamut of crimes from armed robbery to rape!

Almost as if he could divine her thoughts, he smiled, a lingering, insolent smile displaying even, startlingly white teeth, and she realised with a sickening jolt that a man who could exude such a potent sexual attraction, apparently at will, would never need to resort to rape.

He stood up then, head and shoulders taller than any other man in the room, as she could see at a glance, lean and graceful like the jaguars who stalked in the undergrowth. A great silver buckle ornamenting the belt which was slung low on his hips, a silver medallion nestling among the dark hairs on his chest—they were the only touches of colour about him—and she remembered her joking resolution to come face to face with the devil himself if need be, and a little involuntary shiver ran through her.

His smile widened and she realised he had gauged her reaction and was amused by it. She forced herself to stand her ground as he approached unhurriedly round the table and came to stand in front of her.

'I am Vitas de Mendoza, *señorita*. What do you want with me?'

She was sorely tempted to say it had all been a mistake, and beat a hasty retreat. But at the same time, she knew this would accomplish nothing except to make her look a complete fool in front of these men, and that was the last thing she wanted. Her brain worked feverishly, and words rose to her lips.

'I wish to buy your services, *señor*.'

Which wasn't in the least what she'd intended to say, and she saw the dark brows lift mockingly in response.

He said lazily, 'You flatter me, of course, *querida,* but I regret that I am not for sale.'

One or two of his companions laughed, but it was uneasy laughter. Rachel noticed it almost without noticing it, because her face was burning with swift embarrassment at having been betrayed into saying something so ambiguous.

'You don't understand.' In spite of her confusion, she lifted her chin and looked steadily at him. 'I need a guide— a reliable one. You have been recommended.' She was aware of it again—that intangible sense of unease in the room after she had spoken. She said, 'You are a guide, aren't you? The hotel-keeper said. . . .'

'You've been talking to Ramirez?' He broke across her rather stumbling words. 'Well, he's right. I do know this region better than most men, and my advice to you is go back to Bogota and join one of the organised tours. This is no place for a woman.'

He turned away in dismissal.

'No, wait.' Almost before she knew what she was doing, she put out a hand and tugged at the sleeve of his shirt. He stopped and looked down at her hand, and there was a kind of hauteur in his expression. Her fingers looked very white and slender against the dark material, the nails smoothly rounded and painted with her usual pale pink polish. She relinquished the silky material hurriedly, the heat rising in her body as if she had inadvertently touched his skin.

She thought, 'How dare he look like that! He may have a more educated accent than his friends, but he's only a guide, after all. He's for hire. He has to work for his living.'

Something of what she was thinking showed in her tone as she said, 'Perhaps we could discuss this in private. I'm able to pay for your time, if that's what's concerning you.'

'It is not.' His face was expressionless, but she had the oddest feeling he was secretly amused. 'You are a stubborn lady, *querida*, and a reckless one, I think. You should not offer to pay until you know the price you might be asked.'

'This would obviously have to be part of the discussion,' Rachel said. 'Please talk to me about it at least.' She heard the almost pleading note in her voice with a sense of shock. That wasn't what she had intended at all.

'You imagine your powers of persuasion will be more effective when we are alone?' he asked, and laughed as the colour rose in her face. '*Muy bien, chica*, we will talk if you think it will make any difference, but later.'

'We should talk now. This is important,' she said in a low voice.

'To you perhaps,' he drawled. 'But at the moment, nothing is more important to me than my game which you have interrupted—and I have a winning hand. I will talk to you later.'

His hand came up, and his lean fingers stroked her cheek in the merest flick of a caress.

Rachel heard herself gasp, as startled as if he had struck her. Or kissed her.

She whirled round and out of the room, slamming the door behind her for emphasis, hearing the echo of laughter follow her.

The reception desk was once more deserted, but she heard a chink of glasses coming from behind a half-opened door to the right of the entrance and went and looked round it. It was a large room with tables and a bar, empty now except for the man called Ramirez who was polishing glasses behind the bar. He looked surprised to see her and she wondered waspishly if he'd known exactly the sort of reception she was going to get—had perhaps even been listening at the door.

'Your bargain is made, *señorita*?' he enquired, straight-faced.

'Not quite,' she said too sweetly. 'We're going to talk later. I'm afraid that you're going to have to let me have that room after all.'

He gave her another long look. He was probably wondering why she wasn't scuttling back to Bogota, her tail between her legs, she thought angrily.

'Señor de Mendoza said he would speak with you later?' He sounded incredulous, and she smiled kindly at him.

'Indeed he did, after we'd got one or two points straightened out. He seemed to have some strange ideas about why I wished to hire him—and a very inflated opinion of his own attractions,' she added for good measure. But she knew she was being unfair. Vitas de Mendoza was not the sort of man to indulge in illusions, and he could not have failed to know by now that his dark, saturnine good looks and the piratical extravagance of that eye-patch would be the realisation of a thousand women's fantasies. She just happened to be the thousand and first, that was all.

'He has reason,' Ramirez said calmly. He chuckled reminiscently. 'There was one woman—a *norteamericana*—she came here with her husband to see the country. Later she returned alone, and Vitas took her into the hills. They were gone a long time.' He eyed Rachel. 'Her hair was fair, like yours, *señorita*,' he added blandly.

'I can assure you that is the only resemblance,' she said coldly. 'Now can I please see this room? I did not enjoy the journey here, and I'm rather tired.'

He shrugged almost fatalistically. '*Si, señorita.*'

The room he showed her was not large, but it was scrupulously clean, the narrow bed gay with Indian blankets, soft as fleece. They were selling similar blankets on the market stalls in the square below and Rachel promised herself she would buy one. But that would be later. All she wanted to do now was lie down on that bed and try to forget that foul bus journey. There was a bathroom just down the corridor with a small, rather reluctant shower, and she stripped and washed the dust and some of her aches away. It was bliss to come back to her room and put on fresh underwear from her small stock, and lock the door and close the shutters, so that the noise from the square became a muted and not intolerable hum, and then stretch out on the bed.

Yet in spite of her bone-weariness, sleep seemed oddly elusive. Strange unconnected images kept coming into her mind—trees by a river with the darkness of a mountain rising behind them—a man wearing black clothes riding a black horse so that he seemed part of it like a pagan centaur—and a fair-haired woman who stood among the trees with her arms outstretched, so that the man bent out of the saddle and lifted her up into his arms, her hair falling like a pale wound across the darkness of his sleeve. Rachel twisted uneasily, trying to banish the image from her mind, but the horse came on until it was close enough for her to see the rider's face with a black patch set rakishly over one eye. As she watched, the blonde woman moved in his arms, lifting her hands to clasp around his neck, drawing him down to her.

Rachel put out a hand to ward them off. She didn't want to see this. She didn't want to know, but her gesture seemed to catch the rider's eye and he turned to look at her, and so did the woman he was holding, and Rachel saw that the face that stared at her from beneath the curtain of blonde hair was her own.

She cried out, and suddenly the images had gone and she was sitting up on the narrow bed in the now-shadowed room, her clenched fist pressed against her thudding heart. She could see herself in the mirror across the room, the gleam of her hair, and the smooth pallor of her skin, interrupted only by the deeper white of her flimsy lace bra and briefs.

She thought, 'So I was asleep after all.' It was a comfort in a way to know that what she had seen had been a nightmare rather than a deliberate conjuration of her imagination. And she was thankful that she had woken when she did. She picked up her gold wristwatch from the side of the bed and studied it. To her surprise, she had been asleep for over two hours.

She slid off the bed, and put on the beige linen trousers she had worn earlier, with a shirt of chocolate brown silk under the loose hip-length jacket. Her hair was wrong, she thought, waving loosely on to her shoulders. She unearthed a tortoiseshell clip from her case and swept the honey-coloured waves severely back from her face into a French pleat, anchoring it with the clip. It made her look older, she decided, and more businesslike.

She swung her dark brown leather shoulder bag over her arm, and went downstairs. It was very quiet—too quiet, she thought. She went to the room where the card game had been in progress and opened the door. It was deserted, and the table had been cleared, the chairs put back against the wall.

Rachel said furiously, 'Well, I'm damned!'

She supposed he thought he'd been very clever, waiting until she was out of the way in her room to do his vanishing trick. It was his way of saying 'No' without further argument.

She bit her lip until she tasted blood. Well, to hell with him! He might be the best, but he couldn't be the only guide in Asuncion. She wouldn't let this one setback defeat her, and if Vitas de Mendoza was going to feature so prominently in her dreams on such short acquaintance, she told herself defiantly that she was glad to see the back of him.

She turned on her heel, and went out into the evening sunshine. The market appeared to be still going strong, and a group of musicians had even started up in one corner of the square, attracting a small but laughing crowd.

She began to wander round the stalls. As well as the handwoven blankets and *ruanas*, there were also piles of the round-crowned hats the Indians seemed to wear. She would need a hat herself for the trip ahead, she supposed vaguely, but something with a wider brim and shallower crown than those on offer here. There were fruit and vegetable stalls too, where flies swarmed busily, and Rachel averted her gaze with a faint shudder. There was little point in feeling squeamish, she told herself firmly. Conditions would be even more primitive on the way to Diablo.

She was hungry too. Presumably the hotel served meals, but Señor Ramirez had said nothing about their times, which further underlined the fact that he was not expecting her to stay. She could smell cooking somewhere, or was it just her optimistic imagination? A few moments later she had her answer. One corner of the market seemed entirely given over to a gigantic open-air kitchen. Open fires had been kindled and great cooking pots of meat and vegetables suspended over them, while nearby chickens turned slowly on spits.

It all looked appallingly unhygienic, and it smelt mouth-watering. Rachel could resist no longer. She continued her stroll nibbling at a chicken leg. Every second person she met seemed to be doing the same, and surely they couldn't all be going to die of salmonella poisoning, she comforted herself.

She had paused by a stall selling ponchos and was examining a beauty in a wild zigzag pattern of grey and black and red, when a voice behind her said urgently, 'Señorita!'

She turned and saw a small man dressed in a tight-fitting white suit. He had a sallow face and a drooping black moustache, and he was mopping furiously at his forehead with a violently coloured handkerchief.

He said, 'The *señorita* needs a guide, yes? I am a good guide. I will take the *señorita* anywhere she wishes to go.'

Rachel stared at him in bewilderment. For an answer to a prayer, he was not particularly prepossessing, she thought. He was plump and rather shiny and a greater contrast to Vitas de Mendoza could not be visualised.

She said slowly, 'I do need a guide, yes, but how did you know?'

The man made an awkward gesture. 'The Señor Ramirez at the hotel, *señorita*. He said so and . . .'

'Oh, I see,' said Rachel, although actually she didn't. She seemed to have done the disapproving Señor Ramirez an injustice. Or perhaps he just wanted to get her off the premises, she thought cheerfully. 'I want to go to a place called Diablo,' she went on, watching him closely through her lashes for signs of dismay and censure. But there were none.

He merely said, '*Si*, *señorita*. As the *señorita* wishes. And when does she desire to set out?'

'I'd hoped tomorrow,' she said, frankly taken aback.

He nodded. 'I will arrange everything. The *señorita* can ride a horse?'

'Yes,' she said. 'But I thought I could probably hire a Land Rover and. . . .'

He interrupted, shaking his head. 'A Land Rover no good, *señorita*. The tracks are bad, and sometimes there are no tracks. Horses are better. I, Carlos Arnaldez, tell you this.'

'Very well, Carlos.' She wasn't going to argue with him. He knew the terrain better than she did. She was glad she had included some denim jeans in the luggage she had brought with her. And she had seen some soft leather boots on a stall which would be ideal for riding.

She was well pleased when she returned to the hotel an hour later, her new boots tucked under her arm. Carlos' appearance might not be in his favour, but she had to admit that he was efficient. He had taken her to one of the local store-cum-cafés, where they had agreed on his fee for the

trip, and also how much he was to spend on the hire of the
horses and other equipment. She had been a little suspicious at the mention of money, wondering if he thought she
was naïve enough to simply hand over a handful of *pesos*
and watch him vanish with it, never to be seen again. But
he had no such intention, it seemed. He would buy everything necessary, he assured her, and obtain receipts for his
purchases, and the *señorita* could reimburse him before
they set off, if that was satisfactory.

Then he had drunk her health and to the success of the
trip in *aguardiente*, while Rachel had responded more
decorously in Coca-Cola.

She had not told him the purpose of her journey. Let
him think she was just a foolhardy tourist, she thought.
There would be plenty of time for the truth once they were
on their way, and she knew she could trust him.

The reception desk was deserted again when she entered
the hotel, and although she banged on the counter and
called, no one came.

'The perfect host,' she muttered, ducking under the
counter flap to retrieve her key from the board at the back.

It was amazing how dark it had become so quickly, she
thought as she made her way upstairs. Outside in the square
lamps had been lit beside the stalls, and the sound of music
drifted faintly on the evening air, the clear tones of a *flauta*
predominating. The sky looked like velvet, and in the
space around the band people had begun to dance. Rachel
had stood and watched them for a few minutes, but she
had found it suddenly disturbing to be alone and an alien
in this crowd, where everyone seemed to be with someone
else.

Also, her blonde hair and white skin were once again
attracting attention, and she was reminded perforce of the
warnings she had received at the hotel in Bogota about
pickpockets who concentrated on unwary *turistas*.

She unlocked her bedroom door and went in, closing the
door behind her.

She knew immediately that there was something wrong,
and the hairs rose on the nape of her neck. There was some-

one else in the room—the stealth of a movement in the darkness, a faint smell of cigar smoke. Her hands tightened around the boots she carried. They weren't much of a weapon against an intruder, but they were all she had, and if she screamed there was no guarantee that anyone would hear her.

She heard the movement again, and following it another sound—the creak of a bed-spring.

Dear God, was she the one at fault? Had she blundered by mistake in the dark passage into someone else's room? If so, she could only hope they were asleep and she could leave before her mistake was discovered. She remembered Ramirez' remarks about unescorted women. Would anyone believe she had made a genuine error?

Her hand reached behind her, fumbling for the door handle, and then a voice spoke mockingly out of the darkness, freezing her into the immobility of disbelief.

'Are you going to stand there in the dark all night, *querida*?'

There was a click as the bedside lamp was switched on, and Rachel found herself staring at Vitas de Mendoza.

CHAPTER THREE

HE was lying outstretched on her bed, very much at his ease, the half-smoked cigar she had smelt smouldering in the ash-tray beside him. Rachel demanded, 'What the hell do you think you're doing in here?'

He tutted. 'Such language, *chica*! What happened to the cool lady I met downstairs?'

She flung the door open and held it wide. 'Get out!'

'Your countrymen say, don't they, that it's a woman's privilege to change her mind. But do you have to be quite so contrary? A little while ago you couldn't wait to talk to me alone. Now that we are alone and I am prepared to talk, you want to be rid of me.' A smile twisted the corner of his mouth. 'Now that is hardly friendly.'

'How did you get in here anyway?' she demanded. 'I locked my door.'

'Ramirez has a pass-key—naturally.'

'Oh, naturally,' she echoed with elaborate sarcasm. 'And naturally he saw nothing strange in loaning it to you so that you could get into one of his guests' bedrooms.'

His grin widened. 'Under the circumstances, *chica,* nothing strange at all.'

Rachel felt an angry flush rising in her face. Normally, she could hold her own in any interchange of repartee. She could flirt, and she could counter the more pointed sexual teasing that was sometimes levelled at her, but there was something about this man which seemed to paralyse her thought processes and allowed him to get under her guard.

Hot words trembled on her lips, but she bit them back. Not yet, she thought, because she had seen a way in which she could get her own back. If he thought he could treat her completely casually, then he was making a grave mistake. He probably thought she was so desperate to obtain his services as a guide that she would stand for anything. Well, he was going to find out just how wrong he was— but not yet. It might be fun to string him along for a little while—flatter his ego, build him up slowly for the big letdown when she calmly informed him that she wouldn't go to the end of the street with him.

She said, 'Perhaps I owe you an apology, *señor.*' And perhaps I don't, she added silently. 'It was just that I was —thrown by finding someone in my room. I know you said you'd talk to me later, but I wasn't expecting it to be quite as—late.' She spread out her hands and gave a slight laugh, and was pleased to see a look of faint surprise cross his dark features.

And this isn't the only surprise you're going to get, she assured him under her breath. Not by a long chalk!

'That disturbs you?' He reached for his cigar.

'Why should it?' she lied calmly. She fetched the chair from the dressing table and sat down at a safe distance from the bed.

He acknowledged her considered placing of the chair with a mocking inclination of his head.

'Which answers my question,' he murmured. 'And yet, *querida*, you have nothing to fear. I told you downstairs that I was not for sale. Well, I don't buy either—or take by force.'

'How good of you to be so reassuring,' she said sweetly.

'I should not be too reassured.' He sounded amused. 'If I decided I wanted you, you would share this rather cramped bed with me.'

The smile was just right. Coolly amused, and more than a little sceptical. 'You really think so?'

'*Si, querida*,' he said very softly, 'I—really think so.'

Inwardly Rachel was blazing with temper at his calm assumption that she would tamely co-operate if he chose to seduce her, but she did not let her anger show. And she was angry too at the way he watched her, his gaze wandering between her mouth and the three opened buttons on her shirt. She had the strangest urge to fasten the buttons, cover herself up to the throat, but she controlled it. Such an action would be a blatant betrayal of her own awareness of him which she didn't want to admit even to herself.

'I was forgetting,' she said guilelessly. 'You have this "thing" about blondes, don't you? Oh!' Her hand came up to her mouth in well-simulated dismay. 'I shouldn't have said that ...'

He stubbed the cigar out in the ash-tray. 'Ramirez seems to have been busy,' he commented. He sounded almost bored. As he probably was, she decided. The blonde *señora* from the States was now just a memory, and a man like Vitas de Mendoza did not exist on his memories.

He stretched lazily, making her conscious of the lean, muscular length of his body beneath his close-fitting black clothes, then linked his arms loosely behind his head. The lamplight glinted on the silver medallion at his throat.

'Ramirez has been talking about you also, *chica*. He tells me you want to go to Diablo in search of—a brother?'

'Yes, I do.'

He frowned. 'Why is this quest so urgent? He told you of the army patrol?'

'I want to find Mark myself. I don't want anyone else involved,' said Rachel, her heart hammering.

He was watching her again, and why did she have this strange impression that he could see more with his one good eye than most men could with two?

'But then I ask myself why, *querida*,' he said musingly. 'And I do not care for some of the answers that present themselves. Tell me, Raquel, is this brother of yours involved with the *guaqueros*?'

Her hands gripped each other until the knuckles whitened.

'I don't know what you mean.'

He raised his eyebrows. 'No? Then I will explain. *Guaqueros* are illegal emerald miners—men, women and children who search for the elusive green flame of wealth in tunnels that smother them, rockfalls that crush them and rivers that drown them. They all dream of the fortune that will be theirs, but do you know where many of them end up—as corpses in the back streets of Bogota, shot or with their throats cut for the sake of their pitiful finds. They say you can find your way to Santa Isabel where the *esmeralderos* live by the bloodstains. So if your brother is in Diablo looking for emeralds, you had better tell me now.'

It was painful to swallow because her mouth was so dry.

'My brother is a geologist on a post-graduate field trip,' she said at last. 'Whatever he's looking for, it isn't emeralds. The only reason I'm looking for him is because our grandfather is ill and wants to see him urgently.'

And there's nothing in that to interest an army patrol, she told herself. Perhaps there was a reward offered for information about illegal emerald mining, and that was why Vitas de Mendoza was so interested in Mark's activities. Certainly he must have another source of income apart from acting as a guide. The sort of fee Carlos had named would not pay for that expensive silken shirt, or anything else he was wearing, for that matter. Unless his clothes were gifts from satisfied clients, she thought bitterly.

'A geologist?' he said thoughtfully. 'An expert who would know where to look for emerald matrix if anyone did.'

'I suppose so,' she acknowledged, wishing that she had described Mark as a botanist or an ornithologist.

'And he chooses to make his field trip to Diablo,' he went on, still in that thoughtful tone. 'Not the most obvious place, one would have thought.'

She shrugged. 'He had some Colombian friends at university. Perhaps one of them mentioned it to him.'

'Perhaps they did,' he said drily. 'That is what I am afraid of, *querida*.'

Rachel wanted to get away from this topic of conversation. She regretted now giving in to her impulse to have some fun at his expense, to make him believe she had been waiting with bated breath for him to offer her his services as a guide, and then tell him coolly she had made other arrangements. The encounter between them was not going as she had planned at all.

And something else had occurred to her too. He had called her Raquel, as Isabel had done. But he didn't know her name. She had never mentioned it to Ramirez or signed the register, and even Carlos Arnaldez only knew her as Señorita Crichton.

'How do you know my name?' she asked suddenly, uncaring as to whether he recognised her question as a ploy to change the subject.

He shrugged. 'While I was waiting for you to come back, I amused myself by reading your passport. You had left it here beside the bed. It made interesting reading, and the photograph almost does you justice.' He smiled lazily. 'But I looked in vain, *querida*, under "Distinguishing marks" for that enchanting heart-shaped mole you have on your left hip. Were you afraid some inquisitive Customs officer might demand to see it?'

Rachel had the curious sensation that she had been turned to stone.

'You were annoyed at the lateness of my visit,' he went on mercilessly. 'Yet I came to your room earlier—using

Juan's key again. You were sleeping so beautifully that I did not have the heart to waken you.'

Theatre dressing-rooms were by no means private places, and in any case there was a kind of backstage camaraderie between actors of both sexes in which Rachel had always joined without a second thought. Yet the knowledge that this man had stood beside her bed and seen her asleep and next door to naked made her burn with shame. The scraps of lace she had been wearing would have hidden nothing from him.

'Thank you for that at least,' she said, her voice shaking. 'Now perhaps you'll do as I asked originally, and get out of my room.'

He gave her a long mocking look as if he knew all about the torment of rage and humiliation she was concealing behind an impassive exterior.

'You seem to forget, *querida*,' he swung his long legs to the floor, 'you need me.'

Slowly she shook her head, and although the edge had been taken off her triumph by his disclosure, it was still sweet.

'Thanks, but no, thanks,' she retorted. 'I've made other arrangements.' She rose to her feet. 'You aren't the only guide in Asuncion, Señor de Mendoza, and under the circumstances I'd feel safer with someone else anyway. Now please get out of my room and out of my life. I really don't want ever to have to set eyes on you again.'

He was very still suddenly and she knew that she'd got to him, and a fierce joy rose in her. So the irresistible, the indispensable Señor de Mendoza had been rejected at last, and he didn't like it. If anything could compensate for his abominable Peeping Tom act, then it was this knowledge.

He came towards her very slowly, and there was menace in every lithe muscular line of him. She'd told him to go, but she was tempted to run herself. There was more to his look of smouldering anger than slightly dented pride, and she didn't particularly want to know what that additional element was.

His hand closed round her arm, his fingers biting into the softness of her flesh, and she had to choke back a cry.

'Who is this man you have hired?' he asked very quietly and deliberately. 'Answer me, damn you.'

'Let go of me,' she muttered between her teeth. 'You're hurting my arm!'

'I'll hurt more than your arm before I've done with you,' he said in the same deliberate tone. 'Tell me whom you've hired to take you to Diablo.'

'I'll tell you nothing,' Rachel snapped. She bruised easily, and the thought that she would have to spend the next few days with the mark of his hand upon her was an abhorrent one. 'If this is meant to be a demonstration of your *machismo*, then I'm not impressed. I don't respond to bullying.'

'Then what do you respond to?' he asked, half under his breath. 'This?'

The hand that was holding her jerked her forward, and she was stumbling, falling forward against the hard warmth of his body. She wanted to recoil, but she was off balance, and his arms were a prison round her, and his mouth a punishment on hers. No one in her life had ever dared subject her to such a kiss, and she fought him like a wildcat, her fists beating at his chest and, when that didn't work, going for his face with her nails.

She heard him swear, and hoped that she'd drawn blood, but he still didn't release her. Instead his kiss deepened, forcing apart the lips she had kept tightly clamped against him. His mouth was a degradation, but in fighting him she degraded herself as well. It was better, she told herself, to simply endure the loathsome intimacy of his embrace. He would soon grow tired of forcing his kisses on a statue.

But it was one thing to resolve to be passive in his arms, and quite another to carry it through. As if he had guessed her intention, his kiss suddenly gentled. One hand moved to the nape of her neck, stroking it softly, sensuously, and she was tremblingly, tinglingly aware that his other hand had left her waist and was sliding inexorably upwards over her rib-cage to cup her breast. His mouth moved on hers as softly as a breeze, his tongue making a lingering exploration of the outline of her lips.

It was a tantalising contrast in sensation. His fingers felt cool on her bare nape, yet burned through the silk of her blouse. And all she had to do to escape him was step backwards, out of this web of beguilement that his hands and mouth were weaving about her. For her own self-respect, she had to break free.

But her slim body was moving of its own volition, arching towards his in a blind, unthinking response which had nothing at all to do with self-respect, and everything to do with needs she had hardly been aware of up to that moment.

And it was Vitas who stepped back. That was what returned over and over again to shame and torment her when she was alone. That, together with the faint smile which told her that to him a woman's body was no more than a musical instrument that he had mastered long ago, and his parting words before he left the room, leaving her trembling and bereft.

'My felicitations, *querida*. One day you may even learn to be a woman.'

The horses which Carlos had hired for the trip might not be either beautiful or particularly spirited, but they were certainly sure-footed, and that was what mattered in terrain like this, Rachel decided as she drew rein and looked around her.

They had been travelling since sunrise, and already she could feel the protesting ache from her unused muscles. But that was all to the good, she told herself emphatically. While she could concentrate on purely physical discomforts, she could shut the emotional disturbance she had suffered the previous night out of her mind. She really needed to do that. She hadn't slept too well the night before, and had risen that morning feeling raw and heavy-eyed.

She had half expected questions from Señor Ramirez when she had gone down to the vestibule to pay her bill, but he had offered no comment, either on her departure or her choice of travelling companion. She'd intended to offer some sharp criticism of the freedom with which he handed out his pass key, but a second thought convinced her it would probably be best not to refer to it at all, no matter what might be read into her silence.

Carlos had warned her to bring as little as possible, and she had chosen carefully—jeans, and a matching blue denim jacket, shirts and a couple of changes of underwear, all of it now tucked away into a saddlebag, and the rest of her gear and her suitcase left back at the hotel at Asuncion to be collected on the return journey, she had told Señor Ramirez, who had shrugged without smiling, the silent gesture saying more eloquently than any words that he was not convinced there would be a return journey. The memory of it chilled her now in spite of the warmth of the sun on her back.

And it was warm, far warmer than she'd imagined after the misty, almost springlike atmosphere of Bogota, but that was hardly surprising, she supposed. The wild road to Asuncion had wound and lurched downwards all the way, and they were descending still, although they had left any semblance of a man-made road far behind them. There were tracks, showing that other people had passed that way, which was an encouraging sign, Rachel thought wryly. Uncharted territory had no appeal for her. She was not of the stuff of which pioneers were made, and she hoped very much that they would catch up with Mark soon before this journey became any more of a nightmare than it had proved so far.

She wondered idly how far they had come already. She wasn't a very good judge of distance, and they hadn't seemed to be travelling in the same direction for more than an hour at a time since they'd set out. But Carlos seemed to know where he was going, and what he was about, and her only course was to trust him. He seemed to have kept his word over the supplies, and as far as she could judge he hadn't rooked her either, and why she should still have had a vague, lingering uneasiness, she could not have said, only that it was there like the beginnings of a toothache and had been ever since they had set off.

It was the sort of feeling that made her want to ride with her chin on her shoulder, looking back the way they had come, which was nonsense. But even this realisation didn't drive it away, and she thought savagely that she knew exactly whom she had to blame for affecting her peace of mind like this.

They stopped on a small plateau where a trickle of a waterfall emptied itself endlessly into a small dark pool, and there they rested and watered the horses, and Carlos made a fire and heated their midday meal, a tin of vegetable stew followed by a tin of rice pudding. Judging by the contents of the food pack, Rachel realised ruefully that the majority of their meals would probably follow this pattern, and leave her with a chronic digestive problem for the rest of her life.

But not all their meals would be camp meals, she remembered. When she had discussed the trip with Carlos in Asuncion, he had assured her they would use any facilities available along the way. It had been a straw Rachel had grasped at with open relief. She might not know a great deal about South America, but one aspect she was well aware of was that it harboured several varieties of snakes, all of them deadly, and even the remotest prospect of an encounter with one of them made her flesh crawl.

The coffee which followed the meal was palatable enough if rather too strong for Rachel's taste. When she had finished her tin mugful, she emptied the dregs and lay back, her head pillowed on her denim jacket, staring up at the hazy blue of the sky, and the harsh sharply defined lines of the great *cordillera*, its peaks wreathed in cloud. It looked like the lavish backdrop for some extravagantly mounted fairytale, she decided, although no stage designer of her acquaintance would have dared incorporate such exquisitely subtle shades of colouring into what purported to be solid rock.

Against the sky, a bird was circling slowly and purposefully, with deep sweeps of its powerful wings. A condor, she thought, the vulture of the Andes. She had read once that that great wing span was strong enough to sweep a horse and rider from a rock ledge, and she shivered at the thought, sitting up abruptly. There was no fairytale about those faraway heights, after all. There was battle and murder and sudden death, and all the things she least wanted to think about.

It was almost a relief to be back in the saddle once more, and heading down into the valley. It was getting warmer all the time, the air more humid, and the landscape seemed to be changing before her eyes, rocks and dust giving way to lush undergrowth. Trees and ferns reared on each side of the track, forming almost solid walls of greenery on each side which Rachel was glad they did not have to penetrate. Flies buzzed and lunged at her unprotected face, and she brushed them away irritably with her hand. In places the track became so narrow that there was barely room even for the horses to pass along it in single file.

Rachel thought that there had to be a better way to reach Diablo. She felt as if she was being trapped in an everlasting green tunnel. The quiet too was oppressive. Apart from the muffled sound of their horses' hooves on the trodden floor, there was only the occasional harsh cry of an unknown bird or vague rustlings in the undergrowth, revealing the presence of some unseen animal, to break the silence.

Her only consolation was that Carlos seemed to be finding the journey equally trying. His plump form swayed from side to side as his horse plodded ahead, and his shoulders looked bowed with weariness.

Rachel wished she had insisted that they travelled by whatever passed for a road in this region, even if it had meant the trip would take longer, and that she had not stipulated that she needed to reach Diablo urgently.

She moved her shoulders wearily under her thin shirt, feeling a trickle of sweat run down between her shoulder blades as she did so. She was looking forward to reaching the *finca* where they would spend the night. From what she had heard, she gathered that the sanitary arrangements at such places could be primitive, but surely there would at least be a tub and some water so that she could have a bath. Perhaps you never realised how beguiling the ordinary comforts of life could seem until you were separated from them for a time, she thought.

But there was no sign of habitation anywhere round as far as she could see, no telltale drift of smoke, and if any eyes watched them pass from behind the tall waving green fronds, then they were not human eyes, and Rachel was angry at the wave of unease which washed over her at the thought. She was tired, that was all. It was proving to be a long day in the saddle with only that one break at noon— and she hadn't slept well the previous night either. Her mouth tightened in irritation. Wasn't it enough that she was out here on this forest path surrounded by predators? Did she really have to be reminded of that other black-clad, one-eyed predator back in Asuncion waiting to draw gullible tourists into his net?—and there would be plenty who would be quite willing to be so drawn, she found herself thinking with an odd bitterness. The woman from the States who had come back simply to be alone with him for a while would not be the only one by any means. For a moment or two she found herself brooding on the thought, then she gave herself a little shake of irritation. What on earth was the matter with her? she scolded herself. So he'd kissed her. It had been a gesture, that was all, to appease his male vanity, and the fact that she had succumbed to his kiss in a moment of weakness altered nothing. If he kept any kind of record of his adventures, she would be marked down as the one that got away. It was an amusing thought, yet it was not capable of bringing even a glimmer of a reluctant smile to her lips.

She didn't want to laugh about it, she told herself vehemently. She just wanted to drive the whole incident from her mind. Vitas de Mendoza had no place there, or shouldn't have anyway. She had too much else to think about and worry over. For one thing, she had no idea how her grandfather was. For all she knew the improvement in his condition which had so encouraged her before she left for Bogota might have been a temporary thing.

It was ludicrous to think that she had envisaged being on her way back to England by now with Mark safely in tow. And at the back of her mind all the time was the nagging fear that this preposterous journey she had embarked on might be a wild goose chase after all, that saner counsels might have prevailed with Mark and he might have abandoned all idea of going anywhere near the Diablo mine. He might well be a thousand miles away at this moment while she was being bitten alive by insects and frightened out of her wits every time the bushes rustled. People who said that the world of the theatre was a jungle had obviously never experienced the real thing, she decided ruefully.

It was getting late, she realised suddenly. It was no cooler, but the sun was dipping down over the trees. She stared round in vain for some sign of life—a coffee or banana plantation, or a forestry service *cabaña*, but there was nothing, and the forest was forbidding enough in daytime. If darkness fell before they reached their destination, she would probably end up a gibbering lunatic.

In the distance she could hear a familiar sound—the lap of running water. Her tired sticky body tensed with anticipation and she leaned forward in the saddle, trying to peer through the encircling undergrowth to see where the noise was coming from. Carlos had turned and he shouted something back to her over his shoulder—the first words he had uttered in several hours, she thought. She couldn't catch the exact drift of what he had said, but she lifted a hand in response and saw him urge his horse forward, apparently satisfied. Perhaps he was telling her there was shelter just ahead, she thought longingly. A drink and a wash, above all, and then she might even feel able to face another helping of tinned stew and rice pudding. Or perhaps they might be offered something a little more appetising by the people at the *finca*, she told herself hopefully, digging her heels into her horse's side.

The trees thinned, and her spirits rose mercurially. Her

horse's rather ambling gait quickened too as if he was also aware that it was nearing the end of the day and rest awaited them.

It all made the disappointment so much more acute when she emerged from the trees and found that they were on the bank of a river, its waters a dingy brown and moving sluggishly but in little eddies which suggested deep and hidden currents. And that was all—no shelter, no *cabaña*, not so much as a tumbledown shack. Rachel looked around her and saw that Carlos had already dismounted, and was taking the saddle from his horse.

She rode slowly towards him. 'What is this place?' she demanded.

Carlos shrugged rather evasively. 'Is just a place, *señorita*,' he returned, obviously trying to sound reassuring. 'It get dark soon, so we stay here.'

'Here?' Rachel was frankly horrified and made no attempt to disguise her feelings. 'But you said there would be forestry service places—and *fincas*. There's nothing here at all!'

Carlos' round face was suddenly less good-humoured. 'There are such places, but it will take too long to reach them. We need to build a fire—it will be dark soon. To-night we stay in the tent I have brought.'

'A tent?' Rachel echoed helplessly. Nothing had been said by either of them about a tent. And it certainly couldn't be a large one if Carlos had brought it on the packs his own horse was carrying.

An odd feeling of distaste swept over her as she visualised the prospect of having to share any kind of tent, large or small, with Carlos in the middle of this wilderness.

She moistened her lips. 'Nevertheless, I think I'd prefer to press on,' she said levelly. 'I find this sort of country a little wild for camping out in.'

Carlos gave her a sullen look. 'That is too bad, *señorita*. It is far to the nearest *finca*. We should not reach it before morning.'

Rachel felt her heart sink, but her training came to her

rescue and she managed to maintain her cool façade. It suddenly seemed important not to let Carlos know her inward alarm. Besides, her imagination was playing tricks with her again, she assured herself. It was this place—the approach of night and the darkness of the encircling forest. The sinister swirl of the brown water. It was—getting to her. Carlos was just an inoffensive little man who had miscalculated, that was all. Probably she should have made it clear to him back in Asuncion that any form of camping was out as far as she was concerned. If their departure hadn't been so hurried at her insistence, she could have paid more attention to their actual means of travel, got it all sorted out to her satisfaction before they ever set out, but she had allowed her impatience to find Mark to get the better of her.

As if he sensed her inner hesitation, Carlos said eagerly, 'This is a good place, *señorita*. Better we stay here. I make a fire.' His smile was ingratiating. 'You may have the tent, *señorita*.'

Rachel bit her lip. He seemed to have assessed with fair accuracy the root of her uncertainty, and succeded in making her feel foolish. She gave a slight shrug and slid out of the saddle.

Carlos was as good as his word. It was only a tiny tent and soon erected, and before long he had a fire going too, and a can of water coming to the boil on it.

The sun had almost vanished by now, leaving a resplendent sky to mark its passing, and a definite chill in the air. Rachel was glad of the blanket Carlos passed her, and she held it round her shoulders as she sipped at her mug of black coffee. The sticks crackling on the fire and the little darting flames had an oddly soporific effect, she discovered as her eyelids began to droop. She had to make herself wake up, remind herself that the least she could do was lend a hand with the preparation of the supper, such as it was. That she needed too to find out from Carlos exactly where they were and how much this direct but lonely route could be expected to cut off their journey to Diablo. If

only she wasn't so desperately tired! She just wasn't used
to spending so long in the open air. Hot-house flower, she
ridiculed herself.

She wished there was someone with whom she could
share her day's experiences—her sense of awe as she'd
looked up at the high peaks of the *cordillera*, capped with
snow and wreathed in cloud, the glory of this spectacular
sunset, even her fears and apprehensions along the forest
trail. She could build those into quite an amusing story in
the re-telling, she decided, but it would all be wasted on
Carlos. She grinned to herself imagining his blank, uncom-
prehending smile as she poured out her heart to him.

She was so lost in her own thoughts she was hardly
aware of him getting up and coming round the fire, and
when at last she registered his short bulky presence standing over her, she assumed vaguely that he had come to offer
her some more coffee and held out her mug to be refilled.

It went flying, knocked out of her hand, the dregs splash-
ing on to the blanket. Dazed, she looked up and saw for
the first time the real reason for that nagging feeling of unease which had plagued her all day—Carlos staring down
at her with the eyes of a satyr. She tried to get to her feet,
but the folds of the blanket hampered her, and besides, he
was pushing her back again with all the force of his sturdy
body.

His podgy hands were tearing the blanket away, and he
was kneeling across her legs, so that she couldn't move. His
eyes were glazed and his moist full mouth was coming
closer.

Rachel screamed. She'd been taught to scream in drama
school, so why, at this moment when she most needed it,
was the most she could manage a strangled choking cry?
She ought to reason with him, something in her brain kept
repeating numbly. Tell him that if he stopped this madness now, she wouldn't report him to the authorities. That
if he let her go now, they needn't even mention it again.
But at the same time she knew horrifyingly that it was too
late for reasoning, that no threat or promise she could make
would have any weight with Carlos. He was panting

savagely and muttering things in his own language that she guessed somehow were obscenities as his hands tore at her shirt, ripping the buttons off it, and she heard him growl his satisfaction in his throat as he uncovered her breasts. His mouth was wet and greedy as he leaned over her.

She screamed again, and this time the sound came full-bodied and piercing from her throat, although it was stupid to scream when there was no one to hear and perhaps she should have saved her strength for this last desperate struggle.

In the meantime she had nearly deafened her attacker. She saw Carlos draw back, his face mottled suddenly with rage, saw his fist clench and his arm swing back, and found herself praying that the blow when it came would render her unconscious.

The explosion seemed to fill the world. She had closed her eyes to escape from the look on Carlos' face and the sight of that menacing fist, but now she jerked them open again, feeling incredibly the weight of Carlos' body shift from hers. She could sit up, shaking back the mass of tangled hair which her wild ineffectual struggles had loosened. Carlos had rolled off her and was lying very still, staring back over his shoulder. His breathing was hoarse and laboured.

She followed the direction of his gaze and caught her breath in disbelief. In the semi-darkness, horse and rider were so motionless that they seemed to be some fabulous beast from a forgotten world carved out in ebony. She saw the barrel of the rifle the newcomer held glint as it was lowered, and the swift supple movement as he swung himself out of the saddle and walked forward. But Rachel had known at once who it was. It was Vitas de Mendoza.

CHAPTER FOUR

'*Buenas tardes*, Carlos *amigo*.' With one booted foot, he kicked the sullen fire into a blaze. 'Up to your old tricks yet again?'

Carlos began to speak. The words came rushing out, harsh and strident in a long monotonous torrent, and although Rachel could not understand what he was saying, some instinct told her the sense of them, and she wanted to press her hands over her ears and reject the outpouring ugliness. But she couldn't move. She couldn't speak. She felt as if she had been literally turned into stone, and in spite of the heat coming from the leaping flames, she felt as cold as stone.

The hoarse words came to a stumbling halt as Carlos paused for breath, and she realised with an inward start that Vitas de Mendoza was addressing her.

'My friend tells me that you accompanied him here with perfect willingness, *señorita*. Is this true?'

The dancing firelight highlighted the bronze arrogance of his face, making him look like some stern carved image from a time long before the *conquistadores* had set their conquering hand on Colombia and its wealth. Only the starkness of the black eye-patch and the deep sensual curve of his mouth reminded her that he was all too human.

'You are silent, *señorita*,' he remarked after a pause. 'Don't they say in your country that silence means consent? If I have intruded I apologise.'

He lifted a hand to the broad-brimmed hat he was wearing and turned as if to go.

'No, wait!' The words seemed to burst from the tightness of her throat. 'Don't go—please! It—it's quite true, I did come here with this man, but it's not what you think—what he's told you. I've paid him to take me to Diablo, that's all ...' Her voice was trembling as she broke off.

What if he didn't believe her? What had Carlos been saying to him? That she had known all along what was going to happen when they made camp for the night—that she had been a willing participant? But he'd been there—he'd been watching them. He must know the truth. As the realisation of precisely what he had seen came to her, her hands moved automatically to pull her torn shirt across her breasts. Carlos' clutching hands had ripped the delicate lace of her bra clean in half, and most of the buttons of her shirt were torn off and missing, so all she could do was drag the material clumsily into place. When she looked up she saw that Vitas de Mendoza had been watching her fumbling actions, a small grim smile playing about his mouth.

Carlos was speaking again, his voice rising to an angry shout. When he had finished, Vitas turned to Rachel again.

'My friend here is very angry. He says only a madwoman would expect him to take her to Diablo for the wretched fee you agreed upon. That you must have known you would be expected to pay—in other ways.'

'It's a lie,' she said desperately. 'I paid him what he asked. Oh God, I wish I'd never started this—never come here!'

'That,' Vitas de Mendoza said crushingly, 'is perhaps the first piece of common sense I have heard from your lips.' The gun he was holding moved and lifted. Carlos scrambled to his feet staring at the gleaming barrel which was pointing straight at him, bleating something in a high, trembling voice, the beads of sweat standing out on his suddenly sallow face.

Rachel said breathlessly, 'What—what are you going to do?'

He did not look at her, he was staring at Carlos with that same grim smile. He said, 'You are not the first woman, *querida*, to suffer at the hands of friend Carlos. Perhaps I would do the world a favour if I made sure you were the last.'

'But you can't!' Rachel's voice was sharp with horror and disbelief.

'But I can,' he said quite gently. 'I have the means'—the gun moved slightly—'and the will to do it.'

'But I won't let you!' Rachel scrambled up on to her knees. 'It would be cold-blooded murder, and you know it. No country on earth would let you get away with such a thing. And nothing happened—you know that.'

'Yes, I know that,' he said. 'But if I had been half an hour later—what then? Carlos likes to play rough, you know, nor would that have been the end of it. You are no-where near Diablo. My guess is that Carlos intended to take you to meet some friends of his at the Venezuelan border, and that would have been the last anyone heard of you—unless you have friends who make a habit of patronising the *casas de putas* in Caracas or Buenos Aires.'

A deep shudder ran through her body. She'd heard of such things happening, of course, but had always privately written them off as old wives' tales. It had never occurred to her even remotely that such a fate could be hers.

'In spite of that,' she said in a low voice, 'you can't kill him.'

He gave her a long, hard look, then gestured the cringing Carlos to his feet.

'You are a fortunate man, *amigo*. The *señorita* gives you your life. I would not have been so generous. Now on your way. But first—the belt from your trousers, if you please.' As Carlos hesitated, he went on mercilessly. 'Modesty is not a virtue I would have associated with you, little man. Not long ago you were only too eager to remove your trousers in front of the *señorita*.' He snapped his fingers. 'Your belt, and don't keep me waiting any longer.'

As Carlos struggled to obey him, muttering what appeared to be blasphemies under his breath, Vitas continued, 'As you are no doubt aware, there is a small settlement a few miles downstream. A brisk walk in the night air will cool your ardour. And don't let me see your ugly face round Asuncion again.'

He gestured with the gun and Carlos went off at a stumbling run, clutching with both hands at the loosened waistband of his pants as he did so. For a little while, the

sounds of his lumbering, cursing progress floated back to
them, then gradually these died away into the distance and
the night was still again.

Rachel's tense body suddenly relaxed, and as it did so
she knew she was going to be sick. With a little groan she
thrust herself out of the firelight and retched violently in
the shadows. When the paroxysm was past, she lay very
still where she was, trembling from head to foot with reaction. She was dimly aware that Vitas de Mendoza was
kneeling beside her.

'Please leave me alone,' she pleaded in a suffocated voice.
Being sick was bad enough without having this man of all
men to witness her weakness.

'Don't be a fool,' he said almost wearily. 'Drink some of
this.'

He passed her a slim silver flask. Another gift from a
past *enamorador*? she wondered, as she removed the stop-
per and put the flask to her lips. Something resembling
liquid flame coursed down her throat and she thrust the
flask away, gasping for breath, but the trembling seemed to
stop miraculously, almost at once.

She sat up, reaching for the protective covering of the
blanket, and said in a stiff little voice, 'Thank you very
much.'

'*Por Dios!*' He sounded faintly amused. 'What an effort
that must have cost you! Come and sit by the fire and get
warm. At least Carlos attended to the necessities of life
before he tried to rape you.'

Rachel sat and watched as he added more wood to the
flames and refilled the coffee pot. She uttered a faint protest as he began to ladle sugar into the black steaming
brew before handing it to her, but he ignored her.

'You have had a bad shock,' was all he said briefly as he
put the mug into her hand.

It was quite true, she thought as she sipped her coffee
obediently. And the biggest shock of all was his unexpected
arrival.

'How did you know where to find us?' she asked at last.
He had been busying himself, unsaddling his horse, but

now he was spreading a blanket for himself on the other side of the fire.

'It wasn't difficult.' He stretched himself out on it, tipping his hat over his eyes, and reaching for his own steaming mug. 'I had been following you all day.'

'You'd been following us?' Her voice rose incredulously. 'But why?'

'You of all people should not need to ask that, *querida*,' he said lazily. 'Carlos is well known to me, and there were many people who saw you together in Asuncion.'

'I see,' she said, but it wasn't true. She didn't understand any of it. She moistened her lips. 'He—he seemed such a mild little man.' She shivered again, remembering the wet lips and the podgy destructive hands.

'A coral snake seems mild enough as it suns itself on a ledge,' he said drily. 'But approach it, and you will soon discover your mistake, and it can be fatal. As it almost was for you, *querida*. How could you have been so reckless? Anyone you asked would have told you the truth about Carlos, yet you rush into the forest with a man about whom you know less than nothing. Are you always such a fool about men?'

'It was a natural enough mistake,' she said coldly. 'I needed a guide and he approached me. I assumed your friend Ramirez had put him on to me.'

His mouth twisted sardonically. 'Juan may have his faults, but delivering defenceless ewe lambs into the jaws of *el tigre* is not among them,' he drawled. 'On the contrary, he thought you were safely in my—care.'

His slight hesitation before the final word was not lost on her. For 'care' read 'bed', she thought furiously, the old antagonism rising up inside her. She might be forced to be grateful to him, but that was all. It didn't mean she had to like him or his macho, male chauvinist attitude to the female sex.

'How wrong can anyone be?' she shrugged, trying for sweet irony.

He was lighting one of his long, thin black cigars, and the look he sent her was equally ironic, reminding her wordlessly and without effort of that long moment in his arms when her body had wanted more than just his kisses.

Rachel felt the colour rise in her face and wriggled uncomfortably inside her sheltering blanket. She hadn't needed that reminder, or wanted it either. It had just occurred to her that she might well have been snatched from the frying pan, only to be deposited neatly on the hottest part of the fire. Her assailant had terrified her, but was she really any safer with her rescuer?

She passed her tongue round suddenly dry lips. 'And what now?' she enquired with a fair attempt at nonchalance.

He gave a slight shrug. 'We get some rest, and in the morning you start on your way back to Bogota.'

She sat bolt upright, the blanket slipping from her shoulders.

'I am not going back to Bogota. I'm going to Diablo. I've told you—I have to find my brother.'

He smiled thinly. 'Fortunate brother to have earned such devotion. But it alters nothing, *querida*. Diablo is no place for a woman—especially a naïve, gullible child as you have proved yourself to be.'

'I admit I was mistaken in Carlos,' she said hotly. 'But I'm hardly likely to be taken in a second time.'

'No?' He raised his eyebrows. 'Can you say with any degree of accuracy where you are at this moment? I doubt it, even if I gave you the map from my saddle pack. Carlos may have promised to take you to Diablo, but he would never risk his skin near that hell-hole. For at least the past two hours you have been travelling away from Diablo, and you did not even know.'

'But you know where it is,' she said slowly. 'You could take me there.'

'And what makes you think I would be willing to risk my skin either?' He drew deeply on the cigar, watching her above the cloud of smoke he expelled.

She was taken aback. 'But you're a guide. Can you afford to pick and choose the work you take?'

'Sometimes I can. But I'll answer your question with

another, *querida*. Can you afford to pay the price that I might require for my services?'

'I don't know,' she said, her brows puckering. It was an aspect of the situation she had overlooked. Most of her ready cash had vanished with the fleeing Carlos. She would be able to draw on fresh funds in Bogota, she had no doubt, but if Vitas de Mendoza insisted on payment in advance as Carlos had done, then it would mean the sort of delay she was anxious to avoid. 'I—I might not be able to give you all the money now, but on our return ...' She broke off seeing that he was shaking his head. 'Oh, please, you must listen to what I have to say! I really need to get to Diablo as soon as possible. I—I'll pay you whatever you ask—in time—but I dare not haggle over money now. You'll just have to trust me.' She paused again. 'You're laughing at me,' she accused uncertainly.

'A little, it is true.' He contemplated the glowing butt of his cigar, then tossed it into the fire with an impatient gesture. 'I said you were naïve, didn't I, *querida*? You surely did not imagine I followed you today simply to save you from a fate worse than death?'

'I don't understand.'

'Don't you? Carlos understood. While he was grovelling to me, he apologised for laying his hands upon my woman.'

She said in a voice like cracked ice, 'But I am—not your woman.'

'Not yet,' he said softly. 'But you will be, *chica*. Because that is the price I require for taking you to Diablo to find your brother.'

There was a long silence. His words seemed to whirl round and round in her head, making no sense at all. She said at last,

'You—you're not serious!'

'I was never more serious in my life,' he said lazily. 'Why should you doubt it? I may have called you a child, but you're woman enough to know that I want you. You knew that back in Asuncion.'

'I—didn't,' she said lamely, and he threw back his head and laughed.

'I thought you were an actress,' he mocked. 'I hope you play your stage roles with more conviction, *querida*. Imagine, if you wish, that you have just been offered a new and challenging one—as my leading lady.'

'Leading no doubt to the shortest run in the history of the theatre,' she said stonily. 'Thank you, but I'm not interested.'

He gave a slight shrug. 'As you wish. Then we return to Bogota in the morning.'

'You may go where you like.' Her breathing was uneven. 'I'm going on to Diablo—alone if necessary.'

'Oh, you won't be alone for long, *chica*,' he said drily. 'You may even catch up with Carlos. I'm sure he would be willing to come to some new arrangement with you.'

'You bastard!' Her voice quivered.

'*Bravo*, Raquel. You delivered that line with real feeling. But if you mean to shame me into escorting you to Diablo without payment, then your luck has run out, *querida*. I have stated my terms. Now the choice is yours.'

'You're mad!' She hugged her knees with her arms, her body as tense as a coiled wire. 'You must be. After all, you don't need to do this. You—you're very attractive.'

He inclined his head ironically. '*Muchas gracias, señorita.*'

'You could probably get any woman you wanted,' she went on wildly. 'So why do this? All you'll achieve if you force me is to make me hate you forever.'

'What force have I used?' That eye-patch made him look satanic. 'I haven't even touched you. It is all in your mind, like this hatred of yours. But when the time comes, I'll teach you not to hate me, I promise you.'

'Perhaps hatred is too strong a word.' She forced her voice to steadiness. 'It's my indifference you'll have to overcome. I don't think it will please you, Señor de Mendoza, to find yourself in bed with a woman who won't kiss you or respond to you in any way.'

'Is that a challenge, *querida*?' He gave a soft laugh. 'If so, I accept it. English ice against Spanish fire. But will the fire be quenched, or will it melt the ice, I wonder?'

'I've already told you the answer to that.' She drew a deep breath. 'Very well, *señor*, I accept your unspeakable terms. You will take me to Diablo to find my brother for—what? One night, two nights?'

He said with sensual mockery, 'As long as it takes, *chica*. And don't delude yourself that my better nature will triumph, or that I'll permit you to vanish before your debt is paid. It won't, and I shall not.'

Rachel looked away, refusing to meet the intensity of his gaze. The beat of her heart seemed suddenly slow and suffocating as all the implications of his incredible demands came home to her. She had been wanted by men before; she wasn't blind to her own attractions. But there had never been a situation she wasn't able to handle—except for Leigh, of course. She sank her teeth into her bottom lip, remembering that unattractive little episode, and how close she had come to making an utter fool of herself. Was that to be her fate, she wondered sombrely, to be regarded by men simply as a sex object? Would she never meet anyone who would love her as a person in her own right, rather than as a body to be desired? In spite of the hurt Leigh's Ice Maiden story had caused her, she had sometimes hoped that one day she would find a man sufficiently caring and interested in the girl behind the image to discover the truth.

She pulled herself together with a start, mentally giving herself a little shake. What strange byways her thoughts seemed to be taking her down! How could the consideration of Vitas' cynical proposition have led on to thoughts of love? His sole concern was with the satisfaction of his appetites, she thought angrily, and she would not have the slightest compunction in leading him up the garden path. If he imagined for one moment that she would keep to this immoral bargain with him once she was safely reunited with Mark, then he was not only an egotist but a fool as well, and fully deserving of the slap in the face that was coming his way.

His voice cut across the oddly disappointing tenor of her

thoughts. 'It's time we got some sleep. We shall be making an early start in the morning.'

She gave him a swift startled look. The mocking intimacy had vanished from his voice. He sounded cool and practical, and probably that was how he would be until they reached their destination, and she would worry about what happened next when they arrived there.

'You seem surprised,' he remarked tauntingly, getting to his feet in one swift supple movement. He walked round the fire and stood looking down at her. 'Did you expect me to demand part of my payment in advance?'

'No, of course not.' She tore her eyes away from his dark face with an effort.

He laughed and reaching down gripped her arms, pulling her up on to her feet.

'You're too trusting, *chiquita*,' he jibed. 'Haven't your experiences tonight taught you that at least? But you don't have to worry. That's the only lesson you'll be called on to learn—for the time being. When our time comes, you see, I want your undivided attention, unclouded by past fears and alarms, and thanks to friend Carlos I don't think you could give me that tonight.'

She was rigid under his hands. She said very quietly, 'Let's get one thing straight, *señor*. I'm—giving you nothing, either tonight or any night. And now if you'd be good enough to let go of me, I'd like to fetch something out of one of the saddle packs.'

A faint smile twisted the corner of his mouth. 'What do you need, *querida*? A gun, perhaps, to defend your honour —or shoot me with?'

She lifted her eyebrows. 'I may be an actress, *señor*, but I have little taste for bad melodrama. No, I need something far more prosaic—a fresh shirt to replace the one your— predecessor tore.' She shrugged the concealing blanket away from her shoulders and let it drop to the ground. Some men would regard that as a provocation, she knew, but he would not. He would know that she was simply demonstrating her utter and total indifference to him, and she hoped that his masculine pride would be dented a little if not bruised. Besides, if she was honest, she knew that he'd seen more of her when he'd stood over her as she lay asleep in her room at Asuncion. That was another humiliation that she hoped to repay with interest before she had finished.

She went on with studied insolence, 'Just tell me when you've seen enough, *señor*.' She allowed her eyes to widen as if something had just occurred to her. 'Or perhaps you'd prefer me not to change this shirt. Perhaps it would suit your *machismo* better to have me ride into Diablo behind you with my clothes half torn off?' She lifted her eyes, innocently questioning, to his face, and saw just for one satisfied second the reaction she had hoped for—the flash of cold anger, instantly controlled, although his fingers tightened momentarily, bruisingly on the soft flesh of her arms.

'It's a beguiling thought, I admit, *querida*,' he said almost lightly. 'But I think you are mistaken in my image.' His dark gaze matched her own insolence as it lingered on her, frankly appreciating the glimpse of her white skin that the torn shirt afforded. 'Why rip a woman's clothes, when to remove them slowly—between kisses—can be so much more rewarding?' He studied with amused interest the hot wave of colour suffusing her face that his words had induced. 'Don't you agree?'

'I wouldn't know,' Rachel snapped, wrenching herself free and walking towards the tent where Carlos had deposited her personal belongings—a lifetime ago, it seemed.

She was furious to find her hands were shaking as she searched through the pack, choosing a spare shirt at random and shaking it to rid it of the inevitable creases.

She closed the flap on the tent and changed swiftly in the darkness, rolling her discarded garments into a tight ball. It was the first time she had ever put clothes on to go to bed in, she thought, but this entire trip was beginning to contain altogether too many first times for her liking.

In the morning she would throw her torn clothes away or burn them, but there was no way in which she was going to leave the frail security of the tent again that night, although she believed Vitas de Mendoza when he told her that she had nothing to worry about that night at least. But even that had not been prompted by any sense of consideration for her, she reminded herself indignantly. He was merely concerned that her experience with Carlos might have proved too much of a turn-off for her to give him the satisfaction he expected.

Oh God, she thought, clenching her hands into fists, I'm going to make him so sorry! At least I know he's not invulnerable. That crack about his *machismo* really got to him.

Smiling to herself, she wriggled with care into the sleeping bag of blankets. Oh, she would lead him along nicely. She might even let him think she was resigned to the inevitable, but at the same time, whenever she got the opportunity she would plant little barbs—barbs he would remember when she finally gave him the slip under Mark's protection.

Still smiling, she closed her eyes determinedly, trying to shut out a small persistent inner voice that wanted to inconveniently remind her that the last time she had made Vitas de Mendoza really angry, the only vulnerability exposed had been her own, and with well-nigh disastrous consequences.

She shifted uneasily in the darkness. That was something she did not want to think about. Nor did she want to ask herself the disturbing question if her motives for provoking his anger once again were quite as simple as she wanted to believe.

It was the smell of cooking that woke her—a delicious, beguiling smell intermingled with woodsmoke that had her sitting up, her nose twitching in appreciation like a Victorian orphan outside a baker's shop. She had no idea what the smell was, but it was certainly not tinned stew and rice pudding, which was an unmixed blessing. She scrambled out of the tangle of blankets and cautiously lifted the flap of the little tent.

It was very early, she realised. There were still little wreaths of mist around the tops of the trees, and deep shadows where the sun had not penetrated. The air smelt cool and damp and incredibly fresh, a freshness that tingled on her skin and made her shiver slightly.

A few feet away the fire crackled merrily, and Vitas de Mendoza was squatting beside it intent on the fish he was grilling on wooden skewers. Rachel would have sworn that it was occupying the whole of his attention, and she started when he said without turning his head, 'Breakfast is almost served, *señorita*.'

She climbed out of the tent and stood up, smoothing the creases from her clothes with nervous hands. She had slept the previous night better than she expected or even hoped to do, and had woken with a feeling of well-being she was not at all sure she deserved.

Now, as she stood in the sunshine, she found herself thinking that her most justifiable emotion would be apprehension. He was stripped to the waist, his black shirt hanging carelessly over one bronzed shoulder, and his dark hair gleamed with moisture. Clearly he had been for an early morning swim, Rachel realised, resenting her own tousled dishevelment.

'I suppose you caught those with your bare hands,' she remarked, her eyes on the sizzling fish.

'I regret to have to disappoint you, but I used a hook and a line like everyone else.' He withdrew one of the fish from the fire and deposited it on a tin plate, deftly removing the skewer.

'The coffee's ready too,' he went on, indicating the steaming pot. 'Take care not to burn yourself.'

'You think of everything, don't you?' She was aware how ungracious she sounded, but she couldn't help it. Her first delight in the newborn day had curled away like the mist from the trees at the sight of him, dark and lean, the muscles in his shoulders and arms suggesting a latent power. For one blinding moment as she stood there looking at him, she'd known how his skin would feel under her fingers, imagined her hands clasping his back, her breasts

crushed against his torso. She didn't like the images she
had conjured up and she loathed herself and the way they
made her feel. So, he was a superbly made animal. Well,
there had never been any real doubt of that, but it did not
mean she had to react like an animal too.

She accepted the plate and poured herself some coffee.
The fish was wonderful, firm rather pinky flesh, and a faint
flavour of woodsmoke, and for no logical reason she felt her
resentment grow.

She said flatly, 'Would you mind getting dressed? Nudity
in the early morning doesn't turn me on, I'm afraid.'

He burst out laughing, and she glared at him, feeling
she had made herself ridiculous.

'As the *señorita* commands.' He put his own plate down
and sketched a burlesque of a bow before thrusting his
arms into the sleeves of his shirt and tucking it down into
the waistband of his pants. 'If that is how you feel it's just
as well you didn't emerge from your sanctuary five minutes
earlier. Unlike you, I don't sleep in my clothes, and I don't
swim in them either. As it is, I can only hope that I have
not irrevocably disturbed your appetite.'

She sent him a suspicious glance under her lashes, sensing some ambiguity in his words, but his dark face wore an
almost bland expression and she decided she would only
make a fool of herself if she pursued the matter as she half
suspected he was waiting for her to do. Besides, she was
too ravenously hungry to want to argue. After all, she
hadn't eaten since that noontime break yesterday, she suddenly remembered, and her spirits faltered as she also remembered how very different the circumstances of her waking this morning might have been. She went on eating,
moving her jaws automatically, but the edge had gone from
her appetite.

After a while she said jerkily, 'I don't think I—thanked
you properly for arriving when you did yesterday. I want
you to know I am very grateful.'

He finished his last mouthful of fish and tossed the
bones into the fire. His mouth twisted a little as he looked
at her.

'Gratitude, *querida*? That isn't what I want from you.'

Her heart skipped a beat. 'But that's all there is,' she said quickly, too quickly. She put down her plate and leaned forward, looking into the fire which was dying now, avoiding looking at him, letting her pale hair swing like a curtain between them. 'I know that—last night was rather fraught, but we've both had time to think now, and I can't believe you really meant what you said, or that you mean to go through with it.'

'Then you had better believe it, Raquel,' he said softly. 'Because I meant every word.' He paused as if expecting some response, but she sat motionless and silent, her eyes fixed on the fire's glowing embers as if she was trying to hypnotise herself. His voice went on mercilessly, 'I don't share your views on nudity in the morning, *querida*. You look very lovely when you have just woken up, with your hair ruffled and your eyes large and bright with sleep. The prospect of waking and finding you naked in my arms has an almost dazzling appeal for me.'

'No!' The sound came almost strangled from her throat. 'Don't!'

He ignored the pitiful appeal in her voice. 'Yes, I too thought last night, *chica*, but my thoughts didn't run on the same lines as yours. I thought of that black velvet mole on your hip and how much I wanted to press my lips against it.' His voice roughened. 'Hair like honey and skin like cream. A man would have to be a eunuch to look at you and not wonder how you would feel, how you would taste.' He gave a harsh laugh. 'Poor Carlos! He must have thought it was both La Navidad and his birthday when you agreed to ride off with him.'

'Don't you dare mention Carlos to me,' she said raggedly. 'I lied when I said I was grateful to you. You—you're worse than he is!'

He lifted a mocking eyebrow. 'Surely your comparison is a little premature, *querida*. And unfair to poor Carlos, who was hardly given the opportunity to ...'

'You know what I mean!' she shouted. 'And you can just stop making your damned edged remarks as well. They may go down well with your—bleached matrons from Santa Barbara, but to me they're a pain!'

She wanted her words to sting, to get under his guard and hurt him, but he only laughed.

'You're beautiful when you are angry too, *chica*. That cool, composed façade cracks a little and one catches a glimpse of the passion underneath. You will be a rewarding experience.'

'Thank you,' she said bitingly. 'Please don't expect me to feel flattered.'

His mouth slanted sardonically. 'I pitch my expectations of you higher than that. And now, if you have finished your breakfast, we had better prepare to depart. I have saved some warm water for you if you wish to wash yourself. I don't recommend the river. The currents are deep and strong, and there could be other inhabitants who might find that white skin of yours an irresistible lure.'

Rachel reached for the pot of warm water he had indicated and stood up carefully.

'I'm obliged to you for your consideration, of course,' she said with glacial sweetness and patent insincerity. 'But if it ever came to a choice between you and a shoal of piranhas, I'd choose them every time!'

And she turned on her heel and walked away.

CHAPTER FIVE

IN spite of her brave words, Rachel decided it would be more prudent to make use of the warm water for her ablutions. She was an adequate but not a strong swimmer, and the swirling brown river looked curiously uninviting in the bright sunshine. Besides, she had not the slightest desire to parade around in front of her antagonist clad in little more than a skimpy towel.

The wash freshened her, in spite of the cramped inconvenience of the tent, and she brushed and combed her hair,

securing the thick honey-coloured strands in an elegantly
secure knot on top of her head before cramming on her
hat. She had no idea what she looked like, and she didn't
care either, she assured herself ferociously. If she looked
like a fright so much the better. At the back of her mind
lurked a fear that Vitas de Mendoza might choose to exact
payment before they reached Diablo and she could rely on
Mark's protection. In fact the more she thought about it,
the more likely it seemed, because, arrogant as he was,
Vitas must surely know that her brother would not idly
stand by and watch her sacrifice herself. She would have to
be on her guard all the time, she warned herself, buttoning
her shirt to the throat.

Besides, she tried to rally her spirits, if she made herself look as plain as possible and behaved as objectionably
as she knew how, she might even manage to diminish her
attraction for him sufficiently for him to decide the game
wasn't worth the candle and abandon his pursuit of her.
No matter what he might claim, she thought, a man like
Vitas de Mendoza would not want to share his bed with a
woman who made it clear she found him repulsive.

The thought made her smile with satisfaction. She was
rolling up her blankets, however, when a dismaying thought
struck her. At a distance she could loathe him quite cheerfully, telling herself he was everything she most despised
in men, sexually arrogant and monstrously conceited. She
wasn't a declared feminist by any means, but she had no
patience with that brand of *macho* either. But she could not
deny that physically he had the most disturbing and unwelcome effect on her.

Yesterday a man had tried to rape her, an experience
which might have left her scarred for life and which had
frightened and humiliated her. But if she was honest, she
knew that Carlos' pathetic attempt to take possession of her
body had hardly impressed itself on her mind at all. The
really shaming memory which kept intruding upon her was
that of herself in Vitas de Mendoza's arms back in Asuncion, her mouth parted for his kiss, her body straining
towards his in unspoken offering.

She sat back sombrely on her heels, both thoughts and actions arrested by the realisation. She had to face facts. If Vitas began to make love to her, she was going to find it very hard to hang on to her moral sense and her self-respect. Nothing she had shared with Leigh had prepared her in any way for the flame which Vitas had lit in her body. It was as if he had unlocked a forbidden door and shown her a whole new world crammed with sensual delights that some deep, unsuspected part of herself yearned for.

It was essential, she thought, for that door never to open again. At least not with him, she amended hastily, a man who preyed on women, and who had learned the sensual tricks he practised to such effect in a dozen other beds.

Yet why couldn't Leigh have discovered these deeps in her? she asked herself bewilderedly. She'd been a fair way to falling in love with Leigh, and she wasn't in love with Vitas de Mendoza at all.

She started violently as his voice, edged with impatience, came to her through the tent flap. 'Are you going to take all day, Raquel? It is time we were setting out.'

She bundled the blankets together with fingers made suddenly clumsy and emerged from the tent.

His black hat tipped low over his forehead, he looked even more like a bandit or a pirate captain than ever, standing there with his hands on his hips, she thought indignantly. All he needed was a sword, or a brace of silver-mounted pistols.

He was looking her over too.

'Your chaste precautions are wasted, *alma de mi vida*.' His gaze rested pointedly on her shirt, buttoned to the collar. 'I have both my memory and imagination to draw upon. Besides, charms that are hidden are in themselves a provocation—or was that what you intended?'

'I intended nothing,' she replied with dignity, if not complete truth. 'But I don't doubt thât you'll believe precisely what you want to believe.'

He gave her a slight half-mocking bow and gestured

her towards her horse which was tethered nearby, saddled
and bridled for her.

She walked over to the animal and began to talk to it
in a low voice. Its ears flickered and it dipped its head,
questing her hand for the titbits she did not have.

Vitas went past her carrying the dismantled tent. 'We'll
use Carlos' mount for a packhorse today,' he tossed at her
over his shoulder. 'It is not fit for a great deal else.'

'Neither of them are,' she returned wryly. 'But yours
is a beautiful animal. He must have cost a great deal of
money.'

As soon as she had spoken, she could have bitten her
tongue out. She'd merely been following a train of thought,
but it sounded as if she was being snide about his source
of income. But he did not seem either offended or on the
defensive.

'He did, but he has repaid me a hundred times with his
courage and devotion.' He ran a caressing hand down the
horse's neck. 'He was bred on the Llanos where these
qualities are born in the bone.'

'The Llanos?' Rachel queried.

'Our cattle plains. Mile upon mile of grass and scrub
as far as the eye can see—for months as parched as the
desert, and then the floods come. A place, it is said, where
a man can lose his past and find himself in truth.'

'You seem to know a great deal about it.' She watched
him load up the spare horse.

He shrugged. 'It is natural enough. I was born there.'

'Were you ever a *gaucho*?' she asked.

'We call them *llaneros*,' he said. 'Yes, I've driven cattle.
That's when I learned to ride.'

'And now you prefer to herd human cattle round the
mountains?' she asked wonderingly. She gave a little laugh.
'What a silly question! Of course you do. It will be a much
easier life, and the pickings will be better.'

He gave her a dry look, 'As you say, *señorita*,' he agreed,
swinging himself smoothly into the saddle.

She felt an odd disappointment. In a way she had hoped
he would be indignant, and defend his occupation, and his

reasons for choosing it. But perhaps there was no defence
and he knew it.

'Will you ever go back there?' She mounted her own
horse.

He shrugged again. 'It is possible.'

As she drew level with him, she gave him a sideways
look. 'To lose your past?'

'Perhaps,' he drawled. 'Or maybe to find my future.
Who knows?'

Which was hardly an answer at all, Rachel thought
crossly as she followed him along the river bank. When they
reached a place where they could once more ride side by
side, she saw that his face under the shadow of his hat
had become harsh and brooding, and she found herself
wondering if her casual questions had sparked off memories
and even regrets that he had no wish to entertain. She
wondered too what had driven him from the Llanos, and
supposed it must have been poverty or the appeal of town
life.

She would liked to have enquired more closely, but it
seemed as if he had withdrawn in some strange way, and
she dared not interrupt his reverie.

The damp fragrant air of the forest encircled them
once again, and they began to climb slowly but steadily,
the track they were using winding upwards in a series of
dizzying zig-zags. Snatches of a haunting perfume came
to Rachel's nostrils and she wondered which of the unknown plants they were passing it came from. Bottle it and
you could make a fortune in Bond Street, she thought, and
smiled to herself.

They had been riding for about an hour when suddenly
the air around them seemed to become alive with movement and colour, a whirring, vibrating mass of wings.

Rachel reined back her suddenly restive horse. 'What is
it?'

'Humming birds. There are thousands of them at this
level. The conditions suit them.' Vitas' tone was brusque,
but at least the silence between them had broken and he
had recognised the fact that she was alive, she thought,

and immediately castigated herself for inconsistency. She should welcome his silence, whatever the case. She should not want to attract his attention. It was just that the contrast between the almost overwhelming attention he had paid her so far and his present attitude was so marked, she told herself, and it made her uneasy. Just when she thought she had got him taped, he had become something of an enigma.

The soft whirling humming of the birds' wings around them seemed to echo the confusion of her own thoughts. Vitas had ridden on ahead again, and she made no immediate attempt to catch up, deliberately hanging back so that she could absorb more fully the strange alien beauty of her surroundings. The trees were tall here, rearing towards the heavens like proud giants, with shrubs and ferns, many of which she had never seen before, clustered round their bases in a dark web. One thick bush in particular caught her eye, its heavy blossom as bright as flame in the dim light.

'You're not what I would describe as the perfect guide, *señor*,' she commented acidly when she caught up with him again. 'Don't you normally provide your clients with some kind of running commentary on the scenery?'

'You only said you wished to be taken to Diablo, *señorita*,' he drawled. 'Had you wanted a botanical tour, you should have applied to someone else.'

Rachel drew a deep breath. 'My deepest regret, *señor*, is that I failed to do so,' she said silkily.

'And I am beginning to regret, *señorita*, that I didn't leave you to Carlos' tender mercies,' he returned harshly. 'Although his interest in biology was clearly a little too basic for you.'

She bit her lip. It was maddening to begin a sparring match with him, only to emerge the loser. And it was undignified as well, she warned herself. She had played the Ice Maiden role that Leigh had thrust upon her well enough back in London. She'd managed to combine an air of cool enigma with an aloof, even offhand manner, which combined with her slender blonde beauty had contrived to make even the most determined womaniser think twice about approaching her. Yet none of it had seemed to impress Vitas de Mendoza—with the obvious exception of her physical looks. Honey and cream, he had called her, she thought, her cheeks warming with mingled embarrassment and annoyance at the memory.

She made herself say evenly, 'I think perhaps we should declare a truce, Señor de Mendoza.'

He slanted an openly mocking look at her. 'And why should we do any such thing, Señorita Crichton?'

'Well,' she shrugged, rather at a loss, having expected him to accede to her suggestion without comment, 'it occurs to me that as we are forced to be in each other's company for a certain amount of time, we might as well make the best of it.'

'*De acuerdo.*' He gave her a sardonic grin. 'I never intended it otherwise, *querida,* believe me. Are you trying to tell me that you are resigned to your fate?'

'I am talking of the trip to Diablo,' she said stonily. 'Not of what may or may not happen when we reach our destination.'

'You sound as if there is still some doubt in your mind as to my intentions,' he remarked. 'If so, I recommend you to dismiss it, *chica*. Don't delude yourself that I am in ignorance of the schemes for evading my predatory embrace which have no doubt been occupying your devious female mind for the past few hours.'

'I don't know what you mean,' she said haughtily.

'No?' He raised an eyebrow. 'Well, think of this, then, *querida*. What will you do if we get to Diablo and find that your brother is not there after all?'

She gasped and her face paled. That was a possibility the startling events of the last twenty-four hours had made her lose sight of.

His voice went on coolly. 'I give you fair warning, Raquel. I agreed to take you to Diablo so that you could find your brother, but if your brother should not happen to be there, I should not consider the terms of our bargain null and void.'

'But he has to be there,' she said almost inaudibly.

He bent towards her out of his saddle. '*Por que*? So that you can take refuge with him? Do you really think I shall permit that?'

'I don't give a damn what you permit,' she said raggedly. 'I told you back in Asuncion why I want to find Mark. My grandfather is very ill, he may even be dying while I'm here arguing with you. He wants to see him before he dies and I've promised to bring him back. That's the sole and only reason I'm here with you, *señor*. Because time is of the essence, and I need to find Mark fast—if not at Diablo, then at some other place.'

There was a brief almost tangible silence, and then he said between his teeth, 'And what manner of man is this grandfather that he sends a girl on such a mission?'

She gave him a defiant look. 'As a matter of fact, you and he have a great deal in common. He also regards women as having no other function than to look decorative, cook, and be submissive bed-partners.'

'Your culinary skills don't interest me, Raquel, and I look for something more exciting than mere submission from you.'

'Then you'll be disappointed,' she flashed.

'I don't think so.' He was frowning slightly. 'So if the grandfather has these views on the status of women, what are you doing here? You cannot have wished to come.'

'Why ever not?' she questioned coolly. 'Perhaps it hasn't worked out as I hoped, but neither Grandfather nor I can be blamed for that. And I did want to come—because he asked me to. I don't know if you have a family, Señor de Mendoza, but if you do, it can't have escaped your notice that you owe that family certain obligations—and they can't be evaded by running away. Besides . . .' she hesitated.

'Please continue.' His voice was icy. Perhaps her remark about the evasion of family obligations had struck home.

'Besides, it was the first favour Grandfather had ever asked of me,' she said in a low voice. 'The first time he'd really acknowledged that I was a human being, instead of a prettily dressed doll.'

'And that really mattered to you?' He turned and stared at her, his mouth set grimly. 'For that you were prepared to set all other considerations aside? Didn't it occur to you that you could be running yourself into danger?'

'I don't think it did,' Rachel said in some surprise. 'My main consideration, apart from pleasing Grandfather, was the effect it might have on my career.'

'Ah, yes.' He inclined his head slightly. 'Your career means a great deal to you.'

'It means everything,' she said shortly.

'Everything?' His voice sounded derisive. 'You are admirably single-minded, *querida*. Tell me, has there never been a man who has made you feel there might be more to life than acting the lives of others?'

Leigh's face came and went briefly in her mind. Strange how little a wound she had once thought incurable hurt now. Perhaps the damage had been done to her pride rather than her heart.

'No,' she said shortly, 'there's no one.' Now why had she admitted that? she wondered in dismay. It might have been better to admit airily to a string of lovers, some intuition told her.

'But that's enough about me,' she went on hastily. 'What about you, *señor*? Have you a quiet, crushed little wife hidden away somewhere?'

'Why do you ask, *querida*?' he came back smoothly. 'Are you afraid she might find out about you and make a jealous scene?'

'Not at all.' Rachel felt her heart was beating uncomfortably fast. 'Although I should imagine any woman foolish enough to share your life on a permanent basis would have a preponderance of such scenes.'

'In that case,' he said drily, 'it is fortunate that the unlucky Señora de Mendoza is still a figment of your imagination, *chica*. You look almost relieved,' he went on. 'Does the thought of my being married disturb you?'

'Not in the slightest,' Rachel assured him coldly. 'Why should it?'

'Why indeed?' he agreed silkily. His hand came up and took her chin, turning her face towards his. Flushing, she jerked her head away.

'Please don't touch me!'

'That disturbs you also?'

'No, it doesn't,' Rachel snapped. 'I just have—an aversion to being pawed about.'

'Such a fuss about a casual contact.' His lips twisted. 'Would you prefer me to take you from your horse and make love to you completely here at the side of the trail?'

'No!' To her everlasting shame the word was uttered as a kind of strangled yelp.

'Then don't provoke me by pretending you find my caresses repulsive,' he said coldly. 'We both know it is a lie, and you merely make things harder for yourself by repeating it.'

Her cheeks burned, and her eyes filled with angry tears. This was what it had led to, that brief and fatal loss of self-control back in that hotel bedroom in Asuncion. If she had just kept her head—slapped his face even—then she would not be in this sordid impasse. But some dark angel passing over in that moment had made her want him, and made him know it, and it would take every scrap of ingenuity of which she was capable to extricate herself from his clutches. It was almost unbelievable, she thought, that one moment of weakness should have brought her almost to the brink of disaster.

And perhaps the most sobering thought was that she couldn't think of one of her friends who would understand her resistance. Most of them, she knew, would be only too happy after maybe a token protest to submit to his dark attraction, living only for the pleasure of the moment, uncaring what heartache the future might bring. She pulled herself up mentally. Why waste even a moment on such thoughts? Vitas de Mendoza was not interested in her feelings. All he required was her willing co-operation in

bed, and that only for a short time, until his fancy for
her waned.

She felt the colour draining out of her face as she
realised for the first time the way her thoughts were leading her. To a realisation that if Vitas took her, she would
be taken for ever. That for her there could be no transitory
affair, followed by a lighthearted parting. That when her
brief reign as his mistress ended, as inevitably it would,
her heart might not only ache but bleed. That the response
she had been trying so hard to deny would not be merely
making love, but loving. And that in that there would be
no future at all.

Imperceptibly her grip on the reins had slackened, and
when her horse stumbled, she was nearly flung out of the
saddle. It was Vitas who saved her, his arm like a bar of
steel steadying her until she had recovered her equilibrium.

'Dreaming in the saddle, *chica*?' he asked jeeringly.
'That can be a quick road to a broken neck—or perhaps
that is what you hoped.'

She was still half stunned by the realisation which had
come to her, but he would attribute her wide, startled eyes
and parted lips to her near-accident, she supposed. She
rallied herself swiftly.

'Hardly that, *señor*. I'm afraid I can't honestly regard
you or any man as a fate worse than death.'

'*Muy bien*,' he approved with a tinge of mockery. 'But
even a broken collar bone could be an obstacle to my plans
for you, *querida*, so take care.'

A warning, she thought drearily as she gathered up her
reins once more and urged her horse forward up the slope,
that seemed to have come much too late.

They stopped for their midday rest on a stretch of
level ground, shaded by some huge mossy boulders. Vitas
had taken one disgusted look in the saddle packs, then produced some dried soup powder from his own pack. The
mixture that he concocted smelled incredibly appetising,
but Rachel could not bring herself to accept the mug that
he brought her.

'I'm not hungry,' she said half-apologetically, shading her eyes against the glare of the sun as she looked up at him. 'I—I think my near-fall must have shaken me more than I realised.'

It was a poor excuse, but any story would do to camouflage the truth.

'You are ill?' He was frowning. He looked incredibly tall against the sun.

'Oh, no,' she said hastily. 'At least, perhaps just a little. It's the altitude.'

His frown deepened. 'I would not have thought it would have affected you at this level. But don't worry, *chica*. We have no more climbing to do today.'

'I can't say I'm sorry to hear that,' she said wryly. 'Yesterday, it was downhill all the way, today, just the opposite.'

'Our mountain tracks are like that.' He gave a slight shrug. 'That is why it can sometimes take days to journey between places which on a map seem only a little way apart.'

'And will it take us several days to reach Diablo?' This time she did not meet his eyes, and she heard him laugh softly.

'Didn't one of your countrymen once say that it was better to travel hopefully than to arrive, *querida*?' he mocked her. 'I won't spoil the suspense by answering your question. Now drink your soup. We have a long ride before supper.' He set the mug down beside her and walked away.

She stifled a little sigh as she watched him go. She had never felt so confused in her mind as she did at that moment, nor so near to panic. She made herself pick up the mug of soup and sip from it. The warm, savoury flavour seemed to put fresh heart into her, and heaven only knew, she thought unhappily, she had never needed it more.

There was a kind of terrible irony in what had befallen her. She, Rachel Crichton, the cool, the level-headed. The girl who knew what she wanted from her life, from her career, and how to get it. Or thought she knew.

The girl too who knew what she wanted from a man—

knew that the only tolerable relationship for her would be based on respect and liking, physical ardour commingled with companionship. In her ideal relationship there would have to be equality, she had always told herself, and a recognition of herself as a person in her own right, instead of simply a decorative appendage to a successful man.

That was what she wanted for herself, she thought fiercely. Self-respect was what mattered. That was why she had never indulged in cheap, transitory affairs.

Or at least that was what she had always believed. Now, she had to ask herself whether it was not because real temptation had not crossed her path before. Not even Leigh, who had wanted to be her lover, had ever managed to elicit from her the sort of response which Vitas—a stranger—had achieved almost at their first encounter.

The admission might shame her, but it was the truth. From the moment she had set eyes on him, she had been bewildered and a little frightened by her awareness of him as a man—she, whose life was spent in a glamorous world peopled by attractive men. If she'd ever given the slightest impression that she was in the market for some casual lovemaking, there would have been no shortage of eager applicants, she knew. And perhaps one of those casual affairs might have blossomed into something more permanent and lasting. She knew of a number of successful marriages which had been created from such tenuous beginnings.

'But not this,' she whispered under her breath. 'Never this.'

She finished the soup and set down the mug, before rising to her feet and stretching wearily. The long hours in the saddle were tiring, and perhaps her fabrication about the altitude had not been so far from the truth after all. It was good to feel the ground solid between her feet and take a look at her surroundings from her own level. Glancing back the way they had come, she was amazed to see how the high tops of the trees formed an almost impenetrable mass. It was as if they were the first people ever to take this mountain trail. During the entire morning they had not set eyes on any sign of human life other than their own, and the realisation of how completely alone they were gave her an eerie feeling.

Perhaps it wouldn't have been so bad if they'd been able to share the normal camaraderie of two travellers, but that was impossible. There were too many tensions between them for that.

She stared back down into the valley, straining her eyes for the distant glint of water to show where the river crawled far beneath. She would get a better view, she realised, if she climbed up on one of the boulders. Vitas was a little distance away, his back turned, attending to the horses. She was about to call out to him and tell him what she intended, but she stopped herself just in time.

For heaven's sake, she muttered inwardly, I don't need his approval—and there were certainly no difficulties about climbing the rock itself. There were plenty of hand and footholds, and the summit seemed to provide a ledge for her to stand on. She wedged her foot in a crevice, tried it experimentally to see that it would bear her weight and not crumble away, then began to climb.

She was almost at the top, her hand reaching up to grasp the ledge and haul herself up on to the summit, when she heard Vitas shout something behind her. Instinctively she froze, turning her head, to see him racing across the grass towards her. He was carrying a machete in his hand, the sun glinting on its long blade, and for one terrified moment she thought he had gone mad. And then she heard something else, just above her head—a slither, and a low sibilant hiss.

'Don't move, you little fool!' His voice was hoarse as it reached her. 'There could be a snake on that ledge. They choose such places ...'

'There is,' she said dry-mouthed. 'Oh, God, there is.'

The machete went spinning out of his hand to fall a safe distance away. He said, 'Jump. Jump, and I'll catch you.'

She said very slowly, 'I—I don't think I can move.'

'Yes, you can, *querida*.' His voice was harsh and authoritive. 'Just let yourself go. Trust me.'

Rachel wanted to laugh hysterically at the very idea, but no sound came from her throat except a little moan and, without thinking any more, she did as he said and dropped off her insecure perch into his arms. She felt them close around her as he staggered backwards, knocked off balance by the sudden impact. The next thing she knew she was lying on top of him in the grass, and his arms were still holding her.

'Did I hurt you?' she asked awkwardly. She made an abortive attempt to scramble to her feet.

'Winded me a little, perhaps. There is more to you than I thought, *chica*.'

She flushed and made another attempt to struggle free of his restraining arms. 'I'm sorry.'

'But I am not,' he murmured wickedly. 'What were you doing climbing that rock?'

'I wanted to see the view properly.'

'It was nearly the last thing you ever did,' he said grimly. 'You are not strolling in your English Lake District now, Raquel. And your quiet approach would have startled the snake. That is when they are most dangerous—when they are frightened.'

It embarrassed and unnerved her to be lying almost completely on top of him, her face just inches from his. She lowered her gaze and stared almost mesmerically at the silver medallion he wore at his throat. She had thought it was one of the cheap religious medals she had seen for sale in Asuncion, but now as she looked closer she saw that it seemed to be some kind of animal instead, almost heraldic in conception, and she found herself wondering where it had come from. It looked older and considerably more valuable than she had at first assumed too.

'Well,' she said after a pause, with inane brightness, 'I have to thank you once more for coming to my rescue.'

'Graciously spoken,' he murmured, a thread of laughter underlying the words. 'But I was hoping you would express your gratitude in a more tangible way.'

'Oh.' She hoped it was the fact that she was lying full-length which was making it so difficult to breathe suddenly.

'Kiss me, *querida*,' he whispered huskily.

She said with a little gasp, 'No—you can't ask that.'

'Oh, but I can—and I do.' One hand came up and tangled in her hair, propelling her head forward. When their lips were the merest breath apart, he paused.

'Well?' he prompted softly.

Rachel was silent, her eyes searching the harsh planes and angles of his face, noticing how the black eye-patch made a sombre slash against the bronze of his skin. His mouth was firm, its essential hardness somewhat alleviated by the slightly sensual curve of his lower lip, and she could remember—oh, how well she remembered—how it had felt against her own—its warmth, its demand. A long, betraying shiver ran through her, and she felt his other hand slide a long sensuous trail down her back to the base of her spine.

If she wanted to be free of him, all she had to do was jerk her body sideways and roll away from him on to the grass. If she wanted to be free.

'Vitas,' she whispered pleadingly.

'I like to hear my name on your lips,' he said softly. 'Now let me feel my mouth there also.'

With a little inarticulate sound, she bent her head the necessary hairsbreadth, her lips shyly caressing the firm contours of his. She would have drawn back again almost at once, but the imprisoning hand in her hair held her close. His mouth was parting, inviting her to a deeper, more intimate exploration, and she was powerless to resist him. Sky and grass were beginning to swing in a dizzying arc as she fought for her last remnants of self-control.

His caressing hand freed her shirt from the waistband of her jeans and slid beneath to rest against the warm skin of her back. She made a little sound deep in her throat as his hand began to move, stroking, teasing, discovering every sensitive spot along her spine until she moved, pressing herself convulsively against him. His own response was immediate and unequivocal, giving her potent evidence of the desire she had aroused in him in her turn. With one swift, lithe twist of his body, he moved so that she was lying beneath him, their mouths still pressed together as if they would drink each other dry.

His other hand disentangled itself from her hair to stroke her cheek and the curve of her jaw, and then move slowly but inexorably down her throat to the neckline of that primly buttoned shirt. Without haste, he began to unfasten the buttons.

A voice she hardly recognised as her own said, 'No!' And her hands came up to thrust against his chest and push him away from her.

'What's the matter, *querida*?' His voice was husky with that hint of laughter in its depths, but his uneven breathing betrayed him. 'Does nudity in the afternoon also disturb you?'

If he undid one more button then she would be bare to the waist, and he would touch her breasts and kiss them, and she would be totally, utterly lost.

'It's your technique that disturbs me, *señor*,' she said bitingly. 'Don't you think it's getting a little shop-soiled by now?'

She felt the blaze of anger in him and tensed, but his only reaction was to roll away from her, his hands releasing her as if they had been touching something unclean.

'An interesting theory, *señorita*.' His voice was quiet, but there was a note in it which seemed to sear its way along her nerve-endings. 'You'll be given every opportunity to test it out completely when we get to Diablo.'

He got to his feet, brushing dust and blades of grass from his clothes, and walked away to where the horses were waiting, leaving her, crushed and desolate, to stumble to her feet alone.

CHAPTER SIX

RACHEL could hardly believe her eyes when she saw the thin trail of smoke rising out of the trees in front of them. Civilisation, she realised incredulously. Or at least civilisation of a type. Her spirits rose, but there was little else they could do, she thought wryly. Certainly they couldn't sink any further than they had done already after this hideous, silent day in the saddle.

The silence between them as they rode had been an almost physical thing, brooding and full of hostility. More than once she had begun to wish she had never said what she did, but at the time it had been an urgent necessity to stop Vitas making love to her for all kinds of good and sound reasons, which still applied, she reminded herself.

Well, she'd succeeded in part at least. He'd stopped making love to her, but she hadn't managed to deter him from his ultimate aim of possessing her, and that was going to be the really damaging consequence.

He had frightened her, she thought. Frightened her by the way he could make her feel, by his controlled strength when he touched her and that strange gentleness which had seemed to restrain his passion as if he sensed he was leading her down paths which she had never trodden before.

Well, she had killed all that stone dead, she thought drearily. And what could she expect in its place? A soulless taking, she supposed. To be used until his anger and the desire that drove him were satiated. And if his lovemaking had frightened her, then the thought of being the toy of his sexual expertise drove her to the edge of panic.

She found herself wondering what would have happened if she had yielded to each clamouring instinct back there on the mountainside and surrendered to him. They would probably still have been there together, she thought, or if they had decided to continue with their journey, then the silence between them would have been a very different thing. And maybe they would not have been planning to spend the night at the *finca* they were approaching—she had already caught a glimpse of its roof among the clustering greenery—but would have pitched the tent somewhere and slept in each other's arms in its cramped interior.

Her throat tightened ominously and she found she was blinking back tears. Oh God, she thought, this can't be happening to me. I don't want it to happen. I came here to establish that I was my own person, that I was in control. That I'm more than just a face and a body and a mass of jangled emotions. I wanted to prove to Grandfather that I could cope as well as a man if that was what he wanted. And I can't even pretend he didn't warn me, although he can't ever have imagined my landing in a situation like this.

Not that she'd ever imagined it herself. In a way Leigh's Ice Maiden taunt had been a defence behind which she had been content to hide and lick her wounds, and tell herself she didn't have to be ashamed because she was not promiscuous. What nice safe illusions she had harboured about herself! she thought bitterly. Until temptation existed, how much did anyone know about their own weaknesses?

One thing she knew now. If Leigh's lovemaking had ever kindled within her one spark of the flame which consumed her at Vitas' lightest touch, then she would have been his mistress long ago.

As it was, she'd let her own indifference fool her into accepting the image he had foisted on her, and believing that she was immune from passion's arbitrary demands. Now she knew differently, and much good might it do her, she thought bleakly.

They were emerging on to a track which actually looked as if it was used. It was dusty and pitted with stones, and there were the marks where wheels had passed. At the sound of their horses' hooves, a scrawny chicken flew across the road in front of them and vanished into the undergrowth with an indignant squawk, and somewhere up ahead of them a dog began to bark.

A few yards more and they would be in sight of the house, she realised thankfully, as it registered with her just how tired and generally grimy she felt.

From what she could see as they passed it did not look as if the *finca* was part of a large plantation. She could see no signs of large-scale banana or coffee cultivation anywhere. She hoped that the owners would not be too poor, or find offering them hospitality too much of a burden, because she felt as if she might drop out of the saddle with weariness.

Even as the thought came to her, the bushes parted and a man carrying a hoe on his shoulder stepped out on to the road. For a moment he stared at Vitas as if he did not believe his eyes, then leapt forward, his teeth gleaming in a broad grin, uttering a shout that could only have been of welcome.

She watched as Vitas swung himself out of the saddle to return the greeting. The conversation which followed was in Spanish and too rapid for her to catch more than a word here and there, but she guessed that Vitas was being asked to explain why he was there and why he was leading an extra horse laden with baggage. Rachel gathered that he must often use this *finca* as a stopping-off place. The two men walked ahead leading the horses, and she followed on behind, resentment boiling up inside her.

Apart from one brief glance, the newcomer had paid her no attention whatsoever, and Vitas had made no move to introduce her or bring her into the conversation. Whatever they were discussing, their heads so close together, their voices low and serious, had to be man's talk, she thought impatiently.

She caught her breath as the house itself came in sight. It was little more than a shack, with a corrugated iron roof, and a broad rather shaky verandah running its full-length. There was some kind of stove on the verandah and a plump woman was bending over it absorbed in cooking. She wore the cotton dress and all-encompassing overall that Rachel had noticed the women wearing back in Asuncion, and her hair was plaited and wound round the top of her head. At the sound of approaching voices she looked up and gave a little crow of delight, throwing down the spoon she was using and jumping down from the verandah with a fair turn of speed to throw herself into Vitas' arms.

From the doorway Rachel saw two dark-eyed children watching the approaching cavalcade intently. She swallowed. The house barely looked big enough to house the little family. There certainly couldn't be room for them as well.

She reined in her horse and sat staring at the tumble-down building. Vitas came and stood looking up at her.

'These are my good friends Ramon and Maria,' he said. 'They speak no English, so you will have to take my word for it that they welcome you to their house.'

She said in a low voice, 'But we can't . . .'

'We cannot what?' He was frowning, his face, his whole stance grim and unyielding.

'They have so little,' she whispered. 'We can't intrude—take from them.'

'*Por Dios!*' he breathed furiously. 'You are an expert at the insult, *chica*, but you will sharpen your claws on me alone. You will not hurt Maria by implying that her house is not good enough for a haughty *Inglésa*. Now get down from your horse before I drag you from it and administer the beating you so richly deserve!'

Rachel descended hastily, sending him a fulminating glance. So he thought her hesitation had been prompted by disdain instead of concern, she raged inwardly. Well, damn him to hell and back and let him think what he wanted! She walked past with her nose in the air to greet her host and hostess and spoiled the effect by tripping over a stone in the road and nearly falling flat on her face. Vitas stood watching her performance acidly, but Ramon and Maria rushed to her side chirruping with distress, and tugging her towards the verandah and the ancient cane rocking chair which stood there.

And there she was ensconced like visiting royalty while Vitas accompanied Ramon and Maria into the house. If he had private things to say to them, he might as well have discussed them in front of her, she thought crossly. But she had to admit that it was a relief to be able to sit still on something that only moved if she really wanted it to. There was even a fan of sorts on a rickety table just within reach, and she waved it gently to and fro, enjoying the faint draught on her face.

She had lost track of the route they were taking. Its twists and turns and ups and downs combined with her own tortuous thoughts had finally defeated her, but the heat humidity told her they were back at a lower level again. She had closed her eyes, but she opened them again with a start when she felt a light tap on her arm.

One of the children was standing beside her, holding a glass containing fruit juice of some kind.

'*Muchas gracias*.' Rachel accepted the glass, and tried to remember her phrase book Spanish for 'What is your name?' and 'How old are you?' But the little girl giggled shyly, putting her hands over her mouth and backed away.

Rachel sipped her juice. It was amazingly cool, and probably chock-full of germs, she thought pessimistically. But at least a sharp bout of dysentery would be one way of preserving her from Vitas' embraces.

She heard a footfall beside her and all her senses jangled.

He said coolly, 'Maria is going to cook us some *empanadas*, but she wants me to ask you if you would like to have a bath.' He saw her give a startled look around her and went on sardonically, 'You are quite right, of course. There is no bathroom, but there is a tub, and Maria has also offered to wash our clothes.'

'But we can't let her do all this for us,' she protested.

His brows slanted together. 'Why not?'

'I should have thought it would have been obvious,' she said hotly. 'It may be part of your system to exploit people, but it isn't mine.'

'Maria does not consider herself to be exploited,' he said. 'And as for you, Raquel, I warn you now you will pay in full for any further unpleasant insinuations that you make about me.'

She decided to ignore the last part of his remarks. 'I

wonder what Maria feels about that,' she said. 'Of course, as she conveniently doesn't speak English, I can't ask her. But do you really think she enjoys living here in the back of beyond in a house that looks as if it would blow down in the next stiff breeze and—and no proper sanitation?'

'Thus speaks the spoiled child of the affluent West.' He gave her a contemptuous look. 'And yes, she does enjoy it, you cold, selfish little bitch. And do you know why? Because Ramon is her man and her heart belongs to him. Wherever he went, she would follow. Whatever life he led, she would choose to lead also. In your countries of quick divorces, you seem to have forgotten that marriage is a sacrament that lasts until death.'

'It seems odd to hear you preaching about marital fidelity,' she said sarcastically. 'From what I was told in Asuncion, you specialised in married ladies.'

'Then you should not believe all you hear, *querida*,' he returned, too pleasantly. 'You have a tongue like a scorpion's sting. I think I shall be forced to commence your taming with a sound thrashing.'

She got to her feet in one swift, angry movement, oblivious of the fruit juice which splashed on to her dusty jeans.

'You'll never tame me, Vitas de Mendoza, no matter how many ways you think of to degrade me.' She was surprised to hear how steady her voice sounded. 'Because I'm my own person, and I belong to no one else. I can close my mind against you, and nothing that you say or do can reach me.'

He shrugged. 'If the behaviour I have seen recently comes from this "own person" then I am not sure that I want to reach you,' he said icily. 'Do you wish me to tell Maria that you don't want to bathe?'

She bent her head, staring down at the rough planking beneath her feet, fighting a desire to cry. 'No—I'd love a bath,' she said in a low voice. 'Shall—shall I come now?'

'No, she will call you presently.' He turned and went back into the dark interior of the house.

Rachel sank back again on to her chair, her legs shaking

under her. What madness had prompted her to say the
things she had? she wondered in desolation. She had
wanted to hurt him, but all her barbs had rebounded on herself. She sighed. It seemed that no matter what she said
or did, in the end she would be the one who was wounded.

She might still be able to evade his embraces, but even
so there was no use in pretending that she would travel
back to England heartwhole. Even if she was not forced
to share his bed, she knew she would not be able to forget
him. In a matter of days, her life, her ideals had been turned
upside down, and she would have to live with the reality
of that long after she had left Colombia behind.

She had no idea how long she remained on the verandah,
staring into space and seeing nothing, but at length she
roused herself. She stood up, glancing down with distaste
at her sticky jeans. Perhaps she would take up Maria's offer
of laundry after all. And she would certainly take up that
offer of a bath. Surely it would be ready by now? Perhaps
Maria had been calling her while she sat on the verandah
dreaming impossible dreams.

She went into the house and found herself in a large
square room. No matter how primitive the conditions, the
cleanliness was almost fierce, she realised as she looked
around her. The furniture was sparse, and much of it
looked home-made, and the rough walls were covered in
gaudy pictures, some obviously cut from magazines, and
others of a religious nature. On adjacent walls, hectically
coloured prints of the Sacred Heart and Our Lady of
Sorrows glowered at each other.

The room was empty, and she called tentatively. Almost
at once a door at the back of the room opened and Maria
appeared smiling broadly, and beckoning.

Rachel went towards her. 'Donde esta el bano?' she
began doubtfully, but she must have made her meaning
clear because Maria nodded vigorously. She led Rachel out
into a small courtyard at the back of the house, where a
strange utensil rather like an old-fashioned copper steamed
over a wood fire.

For one-panic-stricken moment Rachel thought she

might be expected to climb in and boil gently, but she was reassured when Maria ladled out a generous bucketful and handed it to her, gently urging her this time towards a completely different door.

The house, she realised, was L-shaped, and the foot of the L extended to the rear, providing what she supposed were bedrooms. She gave Maria a doubtful smile and opened the door indicated, taking care not to slop the bucket on to the floor.

She was quite right. It was a bedroom, containing at least two beds, she noticed at a quick glance. And in the middle of the floor was an old-fashioned folding screen. All this and privacy too, she thought, staggering a little under the weight of the bucket.

She rounded the screen and stopped dead. She had been quite right in thinking that it concealed the bath tub. What she hadn't bargained for was that the tub was already occupied.

He was shaving, using an old cut-throat razor, and holding a small hand-mirror in his other hand. The glance he gave her was casual to the point of indifference.

'The fresh hot water that Maria promised me,' he remarked. 'How good of you to carry it in here for her.'

'I didn't. At least I—I thought it was for me,' Rachel knew she was babbling. 'I mean—why in the world did she give it to me when she knew perfectly well you were in here?'

He put the mirror and the razor on the floor beside the tub and rinsed off the remaining lather.

'Maria has a romantic soul. You are travelling with me, so she has drawn certain—premature conclusions about our relationship.' He reached to the floor on the other side of the tub and came up with one of his thin, black cigars, half-smoked. 'The water is getting cold,' he added with slight impatience after a pause. 'The intention is that you should pour the contents of the bucket into the tub. And before you start protesting that nudity at any hour of the day and night disturbs you, may I point out that I am up to my waist in soapy water.'

'Alternatively,' she said, 'I could leave the bucket here and you could fetch it yourself.'

He sighed, blowing out a reflective cloud of smoke. 'I should do nothing of the sort, *chica*. I should shout for Maria, who is doubtless busily engaged heating more water for your bath and cooking our suppers and should not be disturbed. She would think it very strange that you were not prepared to perform this small service for your man.'

Rachel hesitated. She knew what the response would be if she protested that he was not her man. Besides, he had clearly given Maria a very different impression, and to make a fuss about a simple thing like adding some hot water to a bath would only confuse the good woman.

Unwillingly she approached the tub, lugging the bucket with her.

'Do you always smoke in the bath?' she asked acidly as the pungent smoke from his cigar reached her.

'Only when I'm alone, *querida*,' he drawled, and grinned maliciously as a startled blush rose in her cheeks as she assimilated the implication in his words. 'But don't be frightened. There is barely room enough in this tub for me. It would hardly accommodate the sort of games you imagine I have in mind. You can pour your water unmolested.'

She would have liked to have poured it over his head, but it was as much as she could do to hoist the bucket to the edge of the tub.

'I only wish it would scald you,' she remarked vindictively as she began to pour the water into the bathtub.

'Fortunately Maria has not your bloodthirsty nature, nor does she share your poor opinion of me. You had better be careful how openly you display your hostility towards me. Maria was my nurse when I was a child.'

'Your nurse?' She glanced up in surprise as she placed the empty bucket back on the floor. 'Did your mother die then when you were very young?'

'My mother is still very much alive,' he said with a degree of hauteur.

She said, 'Oh—I see.'

But she didn't see. The only explanation seemed to be that he came from an altogether wealthier background than she had concluded. But if that was so, why had he worked as a *llanero*, and why was he now hiring out his services as a guide? It made no sense. Unless, she thought gloomily, he was the black sheep of the family and had been made to leave his home.

'If you intend to stay,' he said coolly, 'then you may as well make yourself useful. You might care to wash my back for me.'

'I'll see you in hell first!' The colour in her cheeks heightened and she took a hasty and indignant step backwards.

'You are a strange product of the much-vaunted permissive society.' He leaned back very much at his ease, watching her speculatively.

'There isn't anything particularly permissive about scrubbing a man's back,' she said shortly. 'I just don't care to wait on you, that's all.'

'Ah, I understand,' he nodded. 'It is then on the prohibited list for the truly liberated woman.'

'You're just being ridiculous,' she snapped.

'On the contrary, *chica*, it is you who are being ridiculous.' He held out a piece of damp sponge to her. 'Wash my back, Raquel, *por favor*. I will do the same for you when it is your turn,' he added, the corners of his mouth twisting sardonically.

'You will not!' She paused. 'Very well, *señor*. I'll wash your back on one condition—that you stay right out of this room while I am having my bath. Is it agreed?'

For a moment he studied her, then he lifted one bare wet shoulder in apparent resignation. 'Very well, *chica*. If it's so important to you, then I agree.'

She took a deep breath, then accepted the soapy sponge and began to rub it across his shoulders. His skin felt cool and damp under her nervous fingers, and as he moved slightly she could feel the play of muscle like steel under silk. She felt dizzy and weak, her legs were shaking, and her mouth felt dry. There was tension in him too, she could

feel it through her fingertips, and somehow she had to
break this silent spell which seemed to hold them both in
its thrall, or she would do something disastrous like sliding
her arms round his neck and bending her head until she
could touch his skin with her lips.

It was the scar that saved her, a long, puckered ridge of
skin running down diagonally from his shoulder blade.

She said with a little gasp, breaking the silence, breaking
the spell, saving herself, 'Oh—you've been hurt! When did
it happen?'

'During my time on the Llanos. We bred bulls for the
arena as well as for meat, and one of them decided to blood
its horns on me.'

'You could have been killed!'

He shrugged. 'It was a glancing blow. I was fortunate.'
He turned his head and looked up at her. 'There are some
who would say I bear a charmed life, *querida*.'

She said with an attempt at lightness, 'Or that the devil
looks after his own.' She returned the sponge to him, and
stood hesitating. Reason and common sense were telling
her that she should make her escape now, but still she
lingered.

She said suddenly, 'Your neck and shoulders are as
knotted as a piece of string. I might be able to get rid of
that, if you'd let me.'

She didn't wait for his reply, but put her hands back on
his shoulders, and began to knead gently but firmly. It was
a knack she'd discovered years before, but she used it rarely.
Sometimes Grandfather had allowed her to stroke away his
headaches, and theatre friends occasionally asked for a back
rub to ease away first-night tensions, but this was the first
time she had ever touched a man that she wanted and it
was a new and painful sensation.

But he was relaxing under the pressure of her fingers.
She could feel that he was.

He said lazily, 'You have hands like butterflies, *querida*,
and the true healing touch. Have you never had training
for this?'

She shook her head. 'Years ago, when I was small, I

thought I wanted to be a nurse, but nothing came of it.' She gave a slight laugh. 'It was probably a good job it was only a passing fancy, because Grandfather would have dug his heels in.'

'He doesn't approve of the nursing profession?'

'He's a real old reactionary. If he'd been around at the time he would probably have done his level best to stop Florence Nightingale going to the Crimea,' she said lightly. 'But he doesn't really approve of any profession for women. I think he only let me go on the stage because everyone told him it was overcrowded, and that I would never actually get any work.'

'Presumably, he was wrong.'

She laughed. 'Yes. I've been very lucky—the right breaks at the right time.'

'And it means a lot to you—this career?'

She was a little taken aback. 'Why—yes, of course it does. And you asked me that before!'

Her hands slowed. But did it mean that much? It was what she did, and she enjoyed it, but if someone told her tomorrow she would never walk on to another set, would she care altogether? It was something she had never seriously considered before.

His fingers came up and gripped her wrist. 'Don't stop,' he said quietly.

Her breath caught in her throat. That sensuous trap was closing round her again, and this time it was no one's fault but her own. Her fingers continued to move rhythmically almost like an automaton's, massaging and soothing, but who could soothe away the dull ache of wanting which throbbed deep inside her? No one except the man who had awoken it, and that must not be allowed to happen, because the pain of ultimate loneliness would be even harder to bear.

She said, hurrying into speech, 'Will you tell me what happened to your eye? Was it another accident while you were a *llanero*?'

She felt him stiffen instantly. 'I'm sorry. Shouldn't I have asked? Don't you like being reminded. . . ?'

'I have a constant reminder,' he said bitingly. 'Each and every time I look in a mirror. And no, it was not an accident. It happened a long time ago, and it was quite deliberate.'

She stood motionless, unwilling to believe what she had just heard.

'Deliberate?' she repeated. 'I don't understand.'

'Then I will explain. Thirty years ago, a politician called Gaitan was murdered in the streets of Bogota. His death led to ten years of virtual civil war—*La Violencia*. And for some the struggle was not merely political, it was just an excuse—an excuse to murder and rob and rape. To grow fat and bloated on the misery of others.' His voice slowed, lowered. 'Such a man was Juan Rodriguez.'

Rachel said, 'If this is painful for you, then you don't have to tell me.'

'Is there ever a way to escape pain? You spoke of the scar on my back as if it mattered, *querida*, but I tell you it is nothing compared to the scar Juan Rodriguez has etched on my soul. The scar of which—this,' he put his hand up to the eye-patch—'is the visible sign.' He paused. 'I was born during *La Violencia*, so I grew up with fear, but when I was nine years old, it seemed to be over. But my father was not so sure. Years before he had made a hiding place near our house, big enough for my mother, my sister and myself. We had heard that Rodriguez was marauding in the vicinity, but the news from Bogota was hopeful, so we grew careless. The army was expected through at any time. They would clear up the remnants of groups like Rodriguez'—that is what we told ourselves. Then, one morning, we saw the smoke from many fires. My father made us go to the shelter. My mother was crying, begging him to come with us, and he promised he would follow. But first there were things that he had to do, he said. We stood there while he kissed us, and gave us his blessing, and I remember how my mother took his head in her hands and looked at his face for a long time, as if she knew she would never look on him again. Then we went as he told us and hid. It seemed to me that we were there for a long time. In the end, my mother and sister went to sleep, worn out by crying, and I crept out and went back to the house.' There was a silence, and Rachel felt a kind of shudder go through him.

'Rodriguez was there with my father,' he went on after a moment. 'He had some information that they wanted, and which he was unwilling to give them, so they had been—playing with him. And I was glad that my mother could not see him then.'

Rachel said unsteadily, 'Vitas—I ...' but he silenced her with a lift of his hand.

'I suppose I must have cried out, because some of his men found me and took me into the room where they were. My father was barely alive, but he saw me, and the look of reproach he gave me still hurts. For himself, he had not cared, but he knew he would not be able to see me in the sort of pain that Rodriguez would inflict, and that he would tell him what he wanted to know. But he was spared that at least, because he died only a moment later.' He paused again. 'Rodriguez was angry. His face had no expression, but there was a little muscle jumping in his temple, and I heard afterwards that was a bad sign with him. I could not stop looking at him. He wasn't more than twenty-five years old, but he had made his name stink in men's mouths. Then he turned to me and said, "So the dead dog has left us his litter. Why are you staring, boy? What do you see?" And I said, "I see the devil." For a moment no one spoke, then Rodriguez laughed, and said, "Look well then, for my face is the last thing you will ever see." And he nodded to one of his men.'

Rachel said unevenly, 'Oh God, you don't mean—he couldn't have ... You were only a child!'

'But a child who knew his face, *querida*,' he said gently. 'Few people who had seen Rodriguez had survived to give an adequate description to the authorities. However—as I told you—I bear a charmed life. They had barely started on me when we heard gunfire and the promised army patrol arrived at last. They found me crouching over my father's body. By then, it was too late to save my eye.'

'How—horrible!' Her voice broke. 'What did they do to Rodriguez when they caught him? Did they hang him? Or is it a firing squad in Colombia?'

He said evenly, 'They have never caught him, *chica*. Oh, they have come close once or twice, but Rodriguez is still alive and on the loose, and one day I will meet up with him again. That is one reason I wear this patch—so he will remember the child whose sight he tried to destroy, and know that his hour has come.' He looked at her. 'That shocks you?'

'No,' she admitted honestly. 'Perhaps it should, but I know in your place I would feel exactly the same.'

'*Bravo, querida.*' He spoke with the old mockery. 'But it would be a pity to thwart my plans for vengeance by permitting me to die of pneumonia in an icy bath. Perhaps you would be good enough to hand me that towel and turn your head for a moment.'

She started. 'Yes, of course—I mean—*no!*' Hurriedly she caught up the towel and tossed it to him. 'Now please stay exactly where you are until I get out of this room.'

He laughed. 'Oh, Raquel, what a mass of contradictions you are! Only a few moments ago I felt your hands like velvet upon me, stroking away my stresses and strains, touching my skin as if you could not get enough of me. Now you are pretending to be the frigid English virgin again. Earlier today, you spat venom at me, yet just now your eyes were full of tears when I told you of my father.'

'Give me credit for some feelings!' She was on her way to the door, but she half turned to answer him indignantly, then spun back again with a little gasp. 'I—asked you to stay where you were!'

'I don't have to obey you, *chica.*' His hands descended on her shoulders, turning her to face him. 'Rodriguez tried to destroy my sight, but he affected none of my other senses, and whether you know it or not, your fingertips gave me a message just now—a message I could not mistake. The same one that your lips gave me earlier today.'

'You—you're imagining things.' She stared wildly at the medallion nestling among the dark hair on his chest. 'I—I must go. Supper will be ready. I'm—incredibly hungry.'

'So am I, but not for supper,' he murmured. One hand slid from her shoulder to cup the nape of her neck under the soft fall of her hair, his thumb moving in small disturbing circles against her flesh.

'You're blushing,' he told her softly. 'And your pulses are racing. You cannot tell me you are embarrassed, because I'm now quite adequately covered by this towel, so there must be another reason. Why don't you stop fooling yourself, Raquel? You're not running away from me, but from yourself.'

'If that's what your egotism wants you to believe,' she said in a small stiff voice. 'Now please let me go.'

'I am not stopping you, *amiga*. All you have to do is walk away.' As if to underline his point, he let his other hand drop from her shoulder. 'Why don't you run?' He bent his head and placed his lips deliberately against the betrayal of the tumultuous pulse in her throat. 'Why don't you?' he whispered.

'I don't know.' It was only a thread of sound, but he heard it.

'But I do,' he told her, and pulled her into his arms, his mouth seeking hers with passionate possessiveness. She yielded at once, her arms sliding compulsively round his waist, her fingers spreading across the broad muscularity of his back. She heard him groan her name against her lips—and then heard the hesitant tap on the door and Maria calling, '*Señor—Señorita! Es la hora de cenar.*'

Vitas gave a long reluctant sigh and put her from him very slowly.

'We cannot keep Maria waiting,' he murmured. He ran a caressing finger down her softly flushed cheek. 'Stay with me while I dress.'

Rachel shook her head, trying to control her flurried breathing. 'I—I can't.' Misery threatened to overwhelm her as she realised how close she had been to total surrender.

'You could,' he said flatly. His face hardened a little as he looked at her. 'But run away if you must.' He turned away with a dismissive shrug. 'I am sorry you will have to wait for your own bath until after we have eaten,' he tossed at her over his shoulder.

'It doesn't matter.' She went to the door, then hesitated. 'You—you won't forget what you promised?'

'To respect your privacy?' He smiled rather grimly. 'No, I won't forget—as long as you don't keep me waiting too long.' He registered the startled look she gave him with a sardonic lift of his brows. 'I may wish to use this room,' he explained.

'Oh—I see. Well, I'll just ask Maria to move the tub into my room,' she said.

His laugh halted her on the threshold. 'You are not staying at the Hilton, *chica*. Maria has only one room to offer passing travellers, and this happens to be it. Tonight you will be sharing it with me—unless you can think of somewhere else to run to?'

He laughed again, and its mocking echo seemed to pursue Rachel as she fled across the courtyard to the lamplit room where Maria and her family were waiting to begin their evening meal.

CHAPTER SEVEN

RACHEL had told herself she would not be able to eat a thing, but when the *empanadas*—golden-brown pastry cases, containing a spicy mixture of meat, egg and capers— were glowingly placed before her by Maria, Rachel found them impossible to resist.

Even the arrival of Vitas a few minutes later, immaculate and more disturbingly attractive than ever in dark close-fitting pants, and an elegantly frilled white shirt which only served to enhance the deep bronze of his skin and the raven darkness of his hair, could not spoil her appetite.

She was aware of him all the time, of course, totally and

exclusively, and from the moment he entered the room. Shakingly aware of his proximity as he slid into his place beside her on the rough wooden bench, his thigh casually brushing hers. And she had little else to do as she ate but to think of him and what the night ahead of her would bring. The language barrier excluded her from the conversation and made her the prey of her own tormenting thoughts, even though Vitas was scrupulous about translating remarks that he thought would interest her.

'It's as well you don't understand any of this,' he remarked once in an undertone as he handed her a platter heaped with warm corn muffins. 'Maria is determined to recall what an angelic child I was, and I am sure you would let your disbelief show.'

Rachel gave a small, forced smile, aware that Maria was beaming maternally down the table at them. She wondered how old Maria was. She could not be in more than her late forties, and her children were still quite young, so she must have been almost a child herself when she was Vitas' nurse.

'She was fifteen when my mother hired her,' his voice said almost laconically in her ear, as if he had divined her thoughts. 'She was the eldest of nine children, so there was nothing she did not know about the care of babies, and the love of them too.' He smiled. 'She would have me believe there is nothing she wishes more than to see her own children grow up so that she can come and take charge of my nursery in time.'

Rachel put down her fork, a sudden constricted feeling in her throat as an image came into her mind of Vitas as a father, his dark face softening to tenderness as he looked down at a white-wrapped bundle in his arms. She had seen earlier how Maria's little boy had run to him as he had entered, and how he had swung the child laughingly up into his arms without a trace of self-consciousness. Up to that moment she had never thought of him as a lover of children, or possessing any of the conventional urges to settle down and raise a family of his own, but now she clearly had to think again. She remembered what he said about the Llanos and how he might find his future there, and wondered if that was where he intended his future home to be.

She still had very little clear idea of his own family
background, but the brief glimpses he had afforded her had
shown her that her first impressions of him had been totally
misleading. He was certainly not an ex-cowboy on the
make, but that did not make him less of an enigma to her.
Besides, a family with a children's nurse betokened a certain degree of affluence, she thought, yet the mere fact that
he had not enlightened her on the subject indicated that it
was not necessary, in his view, for her to know. She would
not be around long enough for it to matter, she thought,
bending her head unhappily.

When the meal was ended, she rose as Maria rose, in a
mute offer to help with the clearing away, and was vehemently gestured back to her seat. Beer was brought for the
men, and for her a glass of what Vitas told her was *guarapo*,
made from fermented cane juice. Its potency alarmed her
and she sipped at it with care.

Maria cleared the dirty dishes from the table and vanished, taking the clearly reluctant children with her—to put
them to bed, Rachel guessed. She was absent for a considerable time, and when she returned, she stood in the
doorway and beckoned to Rachel almost conspiratorially.

She soon discovered the reason. Behind the screen in the
lamplit bedroom, her own bath had been prepared. Maria
drew her into the room chattering volubly, and indicating
by gesture that Rachel should undress and get into the
water. Rachel hesitated. How did she explain to a former
children's nurse who didn't speak a word of English that
she was used to taking her baths without assistance? she
wondered with embarrassment. Apart, that was, from sum-
moning Vitas to act as interpreter, which was the last thing
she was going to do.

She looked down longingly into the gently steaming
water on top of which a few crushed green leaves were
floating, giving off a faintly aromatic scent.

She turned and saw that Maria was standing by one of
the beds, holding her saddle pack in one hand, and in the
other the torn shirt and bra that she had forgotten to burn.

Her face was a study as she held up the ripped garments and she turned a wondering face to Rachel, her dark twinkling eyes suddenly solemn.

'El señor?' Her voice was apprehensive, but her face cleared magically as Rachel shook her head, although she still seemed puzzled. As well she might, Rachel thought, as she began resignedly to unbutton her shirt.

It was heaven to slide down into the scented water and feel it lap the heat and grime of the day away from her body. Maria, busily collecting her soiled clothes from the floor, gave her a smile of satisfaction and approval. Her hands moved in a vigorous mime, and Rachel realised she was offering to wash her hair for her. Now that would be heaven, she thought, her fingers releasing it completely from its loosened knot, as she nodded and smiled at Maria. She sat, her eyes closed, as Maria soaped and rubbed and rinsed, her fingers firm and oddly reassuring as they moved on her scalp. She had a sudden vision of a number of small dark-eyed children with hair like ravens' wings lining up obediently to have their hair washed under Maria's tutelage, and something twisted painfully in her heart as she realised whose children she was contemplating. There would be a wife too in the background. Not one of his casual amours, naturally, but a convent-trained señorita from one of the expensive suburbs in Bogota. Someone like Isabel Arviles, who had never worked or had to work for her living, and would be content to spend her days keeping her face and body beautiful for her husband.

When her shampoo was completed, she allowed Maria to help her out of the bath and wrap a towel around her like a sarong. Then she knelt down at the older woman's feet as she was gestured to do, and submitted to having her hair towelled dry. It was like having all her worries and concerns whisked away, and being allowed to lapse into uncaring, unencumbered childhood again, she thought, and how blissful it would be to be allowed to stay here for ever with her head resting on Maria's comfortable lap.

But already Maria was gently chirruping at her to rise. Rachel got up and went across to where her belongings were strewn across the bed. Her hand reached down for her nightdress and paused. It was not there. She turned over the spare shirt and jeans that remained and her last set of clean underwear to see if it had slipped underneath. It was just a brief lawn shift, after all, hardly taking up any room at all. And she must have left it in her luggage, back at Asuncion.

'*Que pasa, señorita?*' Maria came to stand beside her.

Rachel searched her vocabulary. '*Mi camison*,' she managed at last.

Maria gave the garments on the bed a perfunctory poke as if expecting the missing item of nightwear to leap out and bite her, then patted Rachel reassuringly on the shoulder before vanishing out of the door.

She was soon back, her arms full of a billowing mass of white linen, which she shook out for Rachel to see. It was a nightgown, of an age and design which would have fetched pounds in a second hand clothes shop in England, Rachel knew. High-necked and long-sleeved, it was decorated with what appeared to be handmade lace, and the full skirt seemed to spread endlessly. Apart from a faint yellowing along the creases where it had evidently been laid away as a cherished possession, it was in perfect condition.

Rachel began to protest. It was a beautiful thing, almost an antique, and it deserved to be in some museum case, but Maria would hear none of it. Before Rachel could stop her, the concealing towel had been deftly whipped away, and the folds of cool linen were being tugged over her still-damp hair. Maria reached for the hairbrush which lay on the bed and brushed Rachel's hair until it lay smooth and shining like honey-coloured silk over her shoulders. Then she swept the bed clean of clothes and clutter, and went round the room pinching out the wicks of the lamps until only one remained on the cane table which separated the two narrow beds.

Collecting the damp towels, she went to the door, flinging Rachel a last arch look over her shoulder before she vanished completely.

Left alone, Rachel sat limply down on the edge of the

bed. Bathed, scented, brushed and dressed in white, she had no illusions about what she must resemble—a Victorian bride on her wedding night. And that was one of the funniest jokes she had ever heard, only she had never felt less like laughing in her life.

She spread out the folds of linen wonderingly. It was exquisite material, and a faint beguiling scent hung about it as if it had been stored with herbs. Some Spanish nun had probably made this lace, she thought dreamily, for the trousseau of one of the chaste girls being reared for wifehood in the seclusion of the convent. How shocked the good Sister would be—a painful little smile quivered on Rachel's lips—if she could know it was now being worn by a girl calmly contemplating a night of love with a man she hardly knew. Although that wasn't strictly true. There was nothing calm about her. The humming birds in the forest had nothing on the strange quiverings and flutterings taking place in her abdomen. She wanted Vitas to come into the room and take her in his arms and stop her from thinking.

She stood up. The gown was a little too long for her, completely masking her bare feet, and she held the folds of skirt out a little.

She didn't hear the door opening, but suddenly she was aware with every sense she possessed that he was standing in the doorway watching her.

She looked up at him. He was motionless, almost as if he had been frozen there on the threshold, and he was looking at her as if he did not believe what he saw.

She wanted to make some kind of joke, for her own sake as much as anything, to ease the inevitable awkwardness of the next few minutes, but she couldn't speak. Her mind seemed to have become a blank. All that she was aware of was the ache of wanting him, and the slow unsteady bumping of her heart.

Hold me, she begged him silently. Kiss me. Make it all right for me tonight, even if I regret it for the rest of my life.

He moved at last, walking forward into the room, and kicking the door shut with one booted foot. She felt herself tense, her eyes fixed to his face, as she waited for him to come round the narrow bed to her side.

Only he didn't. He stood on the other side of the bed and began to unfasten his shirt.

He said coolly, 'Get into bed, *chica*, before you catch a chill. And don't forget to turn your back because I've no intention of asking Maria if that incredible garment has a male twin in order to spare your blushes.'

She lay on her side, staring at the dark blank of the window, with its protective netting against insects, trying to shut out the quiet sounds of his movements, the rustle of his clothes as he removed them. She heard the other bed give a slight protesting squeak as it took his weight, then the lamp went out.

For a long moment she lay quite still, not really believing what was happening, and then coldly and stiffly her clenched fists came up and pressed themselves convulsively against her trembling lips.

It was late when she opened her eyes the following morning. She could tell that by the angle of the sunlight across the floor. She sat up and glanced across at the other bed. It was empty, and the blankets were folded back. It looked as if it had not been occupied for some considerable time.

Drearily she pushed her own covers back and swung her legs to the floor. Her eyes felt raw as if she hadn't closed them all night, and yet she knew that wasn't true. She had slept, with vague, discomfiting dreams to keep her company.

Someone—Maria?—had placed a jug of water, now cold, and a shallow tin basin on the table between the beds, and she washed quickly, enjoying the cool sensation of the water on her face and body. She folded the nightdress with great care, and placed it neatly at the foot of the bed. She would not be wearing it again, she thought.

She dressed quickly and went out into the courtyard. A clothes line had been rigged up, and she saw her own things drying in the sunshine, along with garments that clearly belonged to the children. As she stood there hesitating, feeling the heat of the day beating down upon her head, Maria appeared carrying a clothes basket. Her eyes lit up when she saw Rachel and she set the basket down.

'*Buenos dias, señorita,*' she greeted her cheerfully. '*Como esta usted?*'

'*Muy bien, gracias.*' It was the conventional response, but not altogether true, Rachel reflected as she walked forward. '*Er—donde esta el señor?*'

Maria's plump face took on a surprised expression. She obviously expected that Rachel would already know the answer to that, and her reply, accompanied by some excited gestures, was almost incomprehensible, but Rachel thought she was saying that he was not here, but had gone somewhere with Ramon.

She frowned a little. She had expected he would at least be saddling the horses in preparation for the final stage of their journey. She had told him how urgent it was that she should reach Diablo. What could have happened?

She became aware that Maria was offering her breakfast, and made herself smile and nod. She went into the living area of the house and sat at the table while Maria bustled around, preparing a fluffy omelette. It was delicious, and so were the crisp golden balls of maize flour and cheese which accompanied it, which Maria told her were *bunuelos.*

Rachel drank two cups of strong black coffee with her meal and gradually decided she felt more human. In a way, she was relieved that she did not have to face Vitas immediately, for she had no idea what she would say, or how he would react when they did come face to face again. The previous night had been another humiliation, she thought bitterly. So, he hadn't expected to find her covered from throat to ankle in voluminous white linen. Well, she hadn't expected it either, but she couldn't believe that she had looked so repulsive. Clearly the packaging hadn't been exotic enough to appeal to his sophisticated tastes, she told herself. Probably he preferred transparent black lace, which veiled without concealing, and the thought made her feel oddly disappointed.

She saw Maria was watching her furtively, and schooled her features. The older woman was probably attributing her rather wan appearance and heavy eyes to a very different cause, she realised wryly.

She glanced at her watch, and saw with a start of horror that it was almost noon. They should have set out hours before, she fretted. Where was Vitas? What was he doing? In spite of everything that had passed between them, his primary obligation was to take her to Diablo as he had promised.

She wandered out on to the verandah and stood staring up and down the dusty track, but there was no sign of him. Maria had followed her and stood watching, her face creased with anxiety. Rachel gave her a reassuring smile and stole another look at her watch.

She spent much of the next few hours wandering restlessly from room to room, and out into the open air. The time dragged, and her tentative offers of help to Maria were rejected with smiling courtesy. She even tried at one point to rest on her bed, but she tossed so much that she decided it would be better if she got up.

The aggravating part about it was that Maria did not seem worried or even vaguely concerned about the men's absence, and her reply to all Rachel's stumbling questions was a smiling shrug.

In the end, she went and sat on the verandah, rocking herself into a bigger and better temper with every endless minute that passed. It was about four o'clock in the afternoon when it first occurred to her that he might not be coming back.

She put down the fan she had been desultorily using to keep the flies away and sat bolt upright.

My God, she thought, it can't be true. He couldn't—he wouldn't just abandon me here. Would he?

The fact that he had become almost as necessary to her as the air she breathed didn't disguise the other fact that she hardly knew him. She gripped her hands together to stop them trembling, and took a deep breath of humid air.

Perhaps this was how it was with him. So far and no

further. Perhaps the foothills of the eastern *cordillera* were littered with his leavings, all sitting like Patience on a monument and smiling at very little.

Perhaps after a decent interval, Maria would come and break the bad news to her in sign language.

Oh, stop it, she admonished herself. You're being ridiculous. If he was going to leave you somewhere, it wouldn't be with friends of his, especially one who idolises him as Maria obviously does.

But nothing could alter the fact that he had vanished without an explanation, she argued. And his disappearance meant their arrival in Diablo would be delayed by at least a day.

She felt herself flush slightly. Perhaps he had merely decided that he didn't want her any more, and this withdrawal was simply a tacit way of telling her so.

She got up restlessly and went back into the house. Maria was sitting at the table, a battered cardboard box in front of her, and in the face of her tranquil smile, Rachel felt ashamed of her own agitation. After all, Ramon was missing as well, and Maria clearly regarded it as an everyday and acceptable occurrence, and not the end of the world.

Maria beckoned and patted the bench beside her invitingly. She was being asked to go and view whatever Maria had in that box. She felt guilty and ashamed that Maria should deem it necessary to have to provide some sort of entertainment for her, but there was no way in which she could convey these sentiments to her hostess, so all she could do was sit down and pretend to be interested in whatever it was she was being asked to see.

In the event, she did not have to pretend the interest, because the box contained photographs. She was shown Vitas as a baby, Vitas as a strikingly handsome small boy, and Vitas as an adolescent, wearing his new disfigurement with an arrogant courage which tugged at her heart. The contrast between the carefree child smiling at the camera, and the disillusion of the young man, his face already marked by responsibility and suffering, was a bitter one.

There were other photographs too, many of them family

groups, and with Maria's help she had little difficulty in picking out his handsome dark-eyed mother and pretty sister. The picture of his late father affected her most deeply. She felt she was looking at Vitas himself in twenty years' time. There was a picture of them together, Vitas on the back of a pony and his father standing beside him, with a protective hand on the bridle. Rachel saw that Maria's eyes had filled with tears as she handed it over, and guessed it had been taken just before the little family had suffered its harrowing and frightening tragedy.

But it was the photographs of Vitas which occupied her attention fully, and she could not maintain the same interest in the pictures of his sister that Maria displayed with such pride—Juanita's first communion, Juanita's wedding, the baptism of her first child. But she had to admit that she was a pretty girl with soft smiling eyes, and no trace of the cynical, sardonic expression which characterised her brother.

At last Maria, sighing gustily, began to gather her treasured relics together again to replace them in the box. Rachel was helping her to collect them up when she noticed a large manilla envelope lying underneath them. As she picked it up to replace it in the box, she saw the corner of a large coloured photograph jutting out a little way which she didn't remember seeing. It was clearly an oversight, she thought, as Maria had shown her everything else her precious box contained, and she began to pull it out of the envelope.

'No, señorita, por favor!' Maria sounded incredibly agitated suddenly, and she made an attempt to grab the photograph out of Rachel's hands. Instinctively Rachel recoiled, and as she did so, she saw what Maria had not wanted her to see. It was a big glossy enlargement that had obviously been taken just outside the *finca* itself, and it was inevitably another picture of Vitas. Clad in his usual sombre black, he stared coolly and unsmilingly into the camera. But he was not alone. There was a woman with him, blonde and petite, with the expensively well-groomed chic of the rich American woman. But she wasn't looking at the camera with the normal tourist smile. She was looking at Vitas, and if the camera did not lie, it did not pity either, for the expression of naked hunger on her face was unequivocally revealed.

'*Ay de mi, señorita!*' Maria wrested the photograph out of her suddenly nerveless fingers, and stuffed it back in the envelope. She looked flushed and unhappy, and guilty as if she had revealed a secret that was not her own to tell.

Rachel was oddly glad that she and Maria did not share a common language, and that there could be no apologies or attempted explanations or other recriminations. It also meant she could not be tempted to degrade herself by asking Maria about the woman.

She knew all that she needed to know already, she thought. Ramirez had given her the outlines of the whole sordid little episode back in Asuncion. And she could fill in the rest of the details from the photograph itself which, even in the brief glimpse she had had of it, seemed to have etched itself irrevocably on her memory.

So Vitas had brought his American lover here. Well, it made a kind of sense, and explained why Maria had seemed neither shocked nor particularly surprised by her own arrival. Perhaps she was used to acting as lady's maid for his women, she thought desolately, and kept a selection of nightwear for their use.

She rose abruptly and went to the door, staring out at the dusty sunlight with unseeing eyes. There was a tightness in her throat and a burning sensation behind her eyelids. She wanted to throw herself down on the rough boards of the verandah and scream and drum her heels, because the thought of Vitas with another woman, holding her, caressing her, brought a surge of bitter jealousy in its wake.

She had not known she could feel such pain, or care so deeply.

But I'm not the first to feel like this, she told herself, her mind returning remorselessly to the photograph. It had not been taken to mark the beginning of their relationship, but the end, she knew. And if she allowed herself to love him, signified that love by giving herself to him, wasn't that

how it would end for her too—her pain, her hunger and
need answered by his indifference?

She shuddered. It was an unbearable thought, yet it had
to be faced. The only way in which a casual affair could be
conducted, she thought dully, was for both parties to play
it cool, to remain basically lighthearted and uncommitted.
Perhaps that was what the American woman had originally
intended—a brief fling to brighten a dull marriage. But if
that had been the intention, the evidence showed it had
gone sadly awry. The strained face that had stared up at
her lover's coolly impassive countenance had spoken of a
passionate involvement.

Rachel thought, 'But I knew—I've always known how it
would be. I knew on the way here that he had the ability to
break my heart.'

Even now, it would be impossible to escape from him
unscathed, but somehow she had to prevent herself falling
any deeper into his toils—the total involvement with him
that her surrender would inevitably bring.

She wondered bitterly whether it had been the memory
of his blonde *enamorador* which had spared her the previous night. Perhaps his conscience had troubled him at
last, reminding him of scenes and tears and despair which
he would not wish to have repeated.

Perhaps, she thought, she was going to be the fortunate
one who could walk away with her self-respect intact,
knowing that she had never grovelled to him emotionally.

But the thought gave her no sense of triumph, or even
any comfort.

She was running very fast through an endless green tunnel.
Behind her a horse's hooves thudded remorselessly in pursuit, but she dared not look round to see if horse and rider
were gaining on her in case she stumbled. Salvation, somehow, lay up ahead, around the next bend.

But as the tunnel wound on she realised she was in a
trap. There was no way out, because ahead of her reared a
sheer cliff face with one small dark opening. But as she
ran gasping towards it, she saw incredulously that the

opening was getting larger until it became the entrance to a cave, and Mark was standing there. She called to him urgently, begging him to save her, but he was staring at something he held in his hand—something which burned with a vivid green flame like a witch-light—and he did not seem to hear her. She screamed his name again, and at the sound of her voice, the green flame in his hand seemed to surge upwards suddenly and she saw the cave entrance and the rock above it begin to collapse, Mark falling backwards into the darkness, his mouth widening in a soundless scream. She cried his name again in desolation, but the hoofbeats were almost on top of her now and hands were reaching down to seize her, and she began to struggle. Only the hands that touched her were not cruel and predatory, but oddly gentle and a voice she knew was telling her, 'Wake up, *querida*. It's a dream—only a dream!'

She opened her eyes and stayed motionless for a moment, dazed and terrified, unable to distinguish between reality and the nightmare world she had left.

But the reality soon made itself plain enough. She was in bed in her room at the *finca*, and Vitas was sitting on the bed beside her, holding her in his arms. Her cheek was pressed against his bare chest, and his hand was gentling her hair while he murmured something in his own tongue.

Rachel said with a gasp, 'Oh, God, I was dreaming!'

'As I told you,' he said drily.

It was dark in the room. She could only see the outline of him as she pulled away.

'I had to wake you,' he went on. 'I was afraid you would frighten the children if they heard you.'

'Was I making a noise?'

'You were shouting for Mark.'

'Yes.' She hid her face in her hands for a moment. 'I remember now. He was in the most terrible danger. We both were. I must get to him. I know he needs me.'

'What danger could possibly befall an innocent geologist on a field trip?' he drawled. 'Or is it possible you are keeping something from me, *querida*? Something possibly to do with the nature of the—samples he hopes to collect?'

She remembered with a start how careful she had been to conceal the truth about Mark's quest. And remembered something else too. She was sitting up in bed, in Vitas' arms, without a stitch on.

She had not bothered to wear Maria's nightgown because she had believed she would have the room to herself. There had been no sign of either Vitas or Ramon at supper or afterwards, and it was clear Maria was not expecting them back. The bedroom had felt stiflingly hot when she entered it, so she had simply undressed and slipped underneath the blanket.

She shot down under the cover, pulling it almost to her chin, hoping frantically that Vitas would not have noticed her state of disarray in the darkness.

'Of course it's got nothing to do with that,' she said coldly. 'I'm just a little on edge, that's all, after being left to kick my heels around here all day.'

'I thought that might rankle,' he murmured, and she could hear the amusement in his voice. 'But there was no way in which I could take you with me, *chica*. There were things I had to do.'

'Man's work,' she muttered sarcastically.

'As you say. You were sleeping so peacefully when I left yesterday morning that I did not have the heart to wake you and explain. I hope you didn't have too boring a day.'

'Oh, no. It was a laugh a minute,' she said savagely. 'I suppose you're not going to favour me with an explanation as to where you've been. I'm paying for your time, in case you'd forgotten.'

'You are quite right in your supposition,' he returned silkily. 'I do not propose to tell you what I've been doing. As to paying for my time—perhaps I should remind you that no payment has been made as yet.' His voice hardened. 'But I intend to collect something on account right now.'

With one deft movement he tugged the concealing blanket free of her clutching hands and slid beneath its shelter beside her. His arms went round her, pulling her against the warmth of his body and she knew the ecstatic torment of his flesh against hers.

'Your body feels like silk,' he muttered roughly against her ear. 'So smooth, so cool, so beautiful. I want to look at you, *mi amada*. Let me light the lamp and ...'

'No!' Her hands came up, frenziedly beating at his chest, trying to push him away, while she twisted her head from side to side, evading his seeking lips.

'Still so shy of me?' he demanded almost resignedly. His hand pinioned her wrists. 'All right, *querida*, you've made your point. This first time, it shall be in the dark, as you wish. But don't fight me now. Relax, and I will show you Paradise.'

'Let go of me! Leave me alone,' she moaned.

'Don't be a little fool. *Por Dios*, Raquel, what are you trying to do to me?' he asked hoarsely. 'You want me as much as I want you—why not admit it? Or is it that you're afraid I'll hurt you? I won't, I swear it. *Amada*, a man who wants a flower to bloom in his garden must cherish the blossom, and I will cherish you, with every breath in my body, with every fibre of my being. How could I be anything but gentle with you?'

Still holding her wrists in one hand, with the other he began to caress her sensuously, intimately, and she felt the shock of response run through her entire body, invading it with a treacherous sweetness. A strange languor was threatening to overcome her, a languor which invited her to move closer to him, to hold him in her arms, and yield her mouth, her breasts, her entire body to his kisses and his touch.

But she couldn't do that. She had to stop him somehow. She had to fight.

'Tell me you're mine,' he murmured against her lips. 'Say it.'

Desperately, she jerked her head back. 'But I'm not! I— I can't be.' A wild inspiration dawned. 'Because I belong to someone else.'

He was very tense suddenly, and his hands fell away from her.

'You'd better explain yourself,' he said after a pause.

'I lied to you,' she said almost in a whisper. 'I told you that Mark was my brother. Well, he isn't. He's my lover. We're going to be married. We—we should have been married before, only he had to come on this trip, and then Grandfather got sick—and he wanted to see us married before he—before he . . .' She stopped.

Her words seemed to be falling into a silence so ominous she wanted to fling up her hands to ward it off. She felt Vitas move away in the darkness and then there was the scrape of a match as he lit the lamp beside the bed.

He looked down at her and there was no desire in his face, no warmth, just a bleak emptiness which seemed to cut her to the bone.

'You lied?' he said very quietly. 'Why?'

Rachel shrugged, aware that she was trembling violently. 'I thought if I told you the truth, you wouldn't act as my guide.' She swallowed. 'I—I knew you fancied me, and I thought I could use that in order to get to Mark more quickly.'

There was another long silence, then he said expressionlessly, 'I see.' And she wanted to shriek, 'No, you don't! You don't see at all. I can't let you love me because if I do I shall be bound to you for ever, and you don't want that from me.' But she said nothing. She couldn't move either, even to pull the blanket up to cover herself from the growing contempt she saw in his face.

He said almost pleasantly, 'There is a name for women like you, *querida*, but I do not intend to soil my tongue with it.' He threw back the blanket and got out of bed. Through the mist of tears that veiled her eyes, she saw him turn away from her. Then the lamp went out, and his voice came to her again from the darkness.

'I wish your *novio* joy of you.'

CHAPTER EIGHT

THEY came to Diablo the following day, as the late afternoon was beginning to dwindle towards sunset.

Rachel stared about her with a curious feeling of unreality. It was not, in any way, what she had expected. She'd had a vague picture in her mind of a rough mining town based on Hollywood's conception of the old Gold Rush days, complete with sleazy hotels and bars, that was nothing like this narrow ravine with its high rugged cliffs. It looked incredibly peaceful, she thought wonderingly, so why then had Vitas been so reluctant to bring her here—and Carlos too for that matter?

And she remembered too when she had said goodbye to Maria that morning how the older woman's eyes had filled with sudden tears, and how she had traced a swift sign of the Cross on Rachel's forehead. At the time, she had been warmed and touched by the gesture, but now remembrance sent a shiver of apprehension down her spine as if it had been a silent warning.

She glanced at Vitas and saw, puzzled, that he had dismounted and was kneeling at the cliff-edge, looking down. After a while, he took a pair of field-glasses from his saddle-pack, adjusted them with care and took a longer more lingering survey of the solitude below.

Rachel wanted to ask him why he was taking all these precautions when the place was so obviously deserted, but on the edge of speech she hesitated, sensing somehow that this was a place for whispers.

It really was very quiet, she thought, and as the hair lifted slightly on the back of her neck, she wondered, 'Too quiet?' On their way here, the air had been filled with forest noises—the chatter of parakeets and chirping of other birds, the hum of insects—even, once, the unnerving shrieks of a howler monkey—but here there was nothing but a silence which seemed to press down upon her.

She bit her lip, accusing herself of being over-imaginative. She took out a handkerchief and blotted the beads of sweat which had gathered on her forehead and upper lip. There was water down in the ravine. She could see the glint of it through the trees, and she could see the falls which served it too—a great dark sheet of water plunging noiselessly down the sheer face of the rock.

Noiselessly. Mentally, she gave herself a little shake. She was getting paranoid about this!

The shadows of the ravine with its tangle of deep undergrowth looked coolly inviting. She wanted to take off her boots and dabble her toes in the stream, let its freshness pour over her wrists.

She looked sideways at Vitas. What were they waiting for? She wanted to ask him, but the words seemed to stick in her throat. Since the previous night and his final biting comment to her in the darkness, he had barely uttered a word to her, and anything he had said had been curt and to the point.

She tried to tell herself that she should be glad, that it was what she had planned, what she had wanted, but the assurances rang falsely in her ears.

He got to his feet and came over to her. His face was hard and unyielding, his mouth set in grim lines as he looked at her.

'You will stay here,' he said. 'I am going to look around.'

'But why can't I came too?' she protested. 'It's still baking up here, and there's shade down in the ravine. I would rather . . .'

'Your preferences are of no account,' he said harshly. 'You will obey me by staying here, or I swear I will make you sorry.'

'But how long will you be?' In spite of herself she heard her voice tremble.

'As long as it takes.' His expression was completely inimical, and she knew she dared not press him further.

She watched him re-mount and swing his horse towards

the clustering trees, and a sense of panic overwhelmed her. She wanted to cry out to him not to leave her, but she knew if she did any such thing, she would only make a fool of herself.

When his tall dark figure had finally disappeared, she busied herself tethering her patient horse in the shade. Then she found herself a convenient tree with spreading branches and sank down at its foot, leaning her back gratefully against its gnarled trunk, and fanning herself gently with her hat.

Whatever her personal unhappiness, it had to take second place to a more pressing problem. Mark was clearly not here, if, in fact, he had ever managed to find his way to this desolate piece of wilderness. Rachel doubted whether she would ever have found it herself without Vitas' guidance. He seemed to know every inch of this wild place like the back of his hand.

She sighed and rested her chin on her folded hands. It seemed as if this whole desperate journey had been for nothing, and she was as far from discovering her brother's whereabouts as ever. In fact the sum total of her discoveries since she had come to Colombia had been about herself, she thought achingly, and none of them were likely to bring her happiness.

She closed her eyes. But that was not what she had to think about. She had to plan—to decide what her next move in tracing Mark must be. She supposed the sensible thing would be to return to Bogota and ask the friendly Arviles family if they had heard anything from him. She would get in touch with Dr Kingston as well, in case by some miracle he had returned to England of his own accord.

That was where she must concentrate her thoughts, her energies—in finding Mark, not sighing after a man whose attitude had shown her plainly that his brief passion for her had burned itself out in disgust and contempt.

When she opened her eyes again it was almost dark, and she was cramped and uncomfortable huddled under her tree. I've been dozing, she thought in sudden panic, getting rather unsteadily to her feet, but for how long? And where is Vitas?

She strained her ears for even the vaguest sound of his return, but the eerie silence seemed to mock her. She shivered a little, clasping her arms across her body. After the suffocating heat of the day, the night came as an almost chilling contrast. She looked at her watch and saw to her vexation that it had stopped. In all the emotional turmoil of the previous night, she had forgotten to wind it.

The question was when Vitas had ordered her to wait there for him, exactly how long had he intended her to wait? He surely didn't intend that she should spend the entire night alone on the clifftop. If people had mined at Diablo, she reasoned, then they must have constructed some kind of shelter for themselves, probably further up the ravine. And if she stayed here much longer weighing up the pros and cons, it would be too dark to make her way down there. As it was, it would not be easy.

She collected her flask of water and the parcel of food which Maria had pressed upon her and began to descend slowly and with infinite care towards the glimmer of water.

She was breathless and shaking by the time she reached the bottom. The descent had been more perilous than she had realised, and in daylight she would probably not have undertaken it at all without help. She stood still for a moment, steadying herself, then she began to make her way carefully along the ravine, using the stream to guide her.

If by some remote chance there was anyone around, they would have heard her coming by now, she thought, stumbling slightly. It was unnerving to think that there might be unseen eyes charting her progress in the gloom, but if there was someone there surely he would have given some sign of his presence by now.

In a way, she thought, as the silence seemed to wrap her round, she would have preferred the Wild West mining camp, clip joints and all.

She was so intent on keeping her balance that she hardly

noticed the white wall until it loomed out of the darkness in front of her. She stopped dead and stared up at it. What in the world? she thought. It wasn't a very high wall, and its crumbling lines were interrupted by a gate surmounted by a small cupola shape. A bell tower, she asked herself dazedly, in this wilderness? To summon whom—and to what?

The gate was hanging off its hinges, its timbers warped and rotting. She edged round it and found herself in what had once been a courtyard. Stones had been laid to pave it, but now weeds and plants were beginning to grow in the cracks between, forcing the stones out of their civilised alignment in a mute warning of the power of the wilderness. A long low white building bordered three sides of the courtyard, the gate wall providing the fourth side of the square. There was something familiar about the shape, and about the arched walkway which separated the building itself from the courtyard, and Rachel thought, 'Of course—it's a cloister.'

Even in what little remained of the light, she could see it was a dilapidated cloister. The order which had built it must have left long ago, she thought, viewing the gaping holes in the tiled roof, and the arches which had collapsed, leaving heaps of shattered masonry to mark their passing.

She had a sudden urge to retreat, to leave this sad place to the ghosts of whatever priests—brothers—nuns—haunted it. But she told herself she was being ridiculous. She needed shelter for the night, and this was shelter, of a sort.

She made herself walk forward, her boots sounding noisily over the flagstones. Just ahead of her, a small night creature scuttled away in alarm, its body a faint blur in the shadows.

Rachel paused, her heart bumping. 'Thank you and goodnight,' she said aloud. The sound of her own voice unaccountably lifted her spirits, making her realise just how much the prolonged silence had been getting on her nerves. Not that she minded things being peaceful—on the contrary. But there was something unnatural about this quietness as though everything that moved and lived was holding its breath in anticipation of some disaster.

She called out clearly, 'Hello—is anyone there?' And like an answering echo, she thought she heard a muffled groan somewhere close by.

She swallowed. 'Vitas?' she queried. 'Is that you?'

Could he have been injured, in a fall from his horse, maybe, and have been lying there all this time waiting for her to come and find him? He seemed an expert horseman, but mishaps could happen to the best of them.

She began to make her way in the direction she thought the sound had come from, stepping into the full shadow of the cloister. She glanced up at the arch a little doubtfully, wondering whether it too was nearing the point of collapse, but it seemed sturdy enough. There seemed to be a number of little rooms opening off the cloister, with gratings set in their doors—rather like a small jail. She supposed this was where the brothers had their cells, where they slept and meditated. She stood on tiptoe and peeped through one grating and her action was greeted with a sudden, startled beating of wings—from a bird, she thought—or even a bat, and stepped back quickly.

It was then she heard the muffled groan again, and she knew without doubt that it came from the next cell along. She moved towards it, her palms suddenly clammy, and peered through the grating. The small room seemed full of lumber, but there was a rough bed against one wall, and she could see a shape lying on it covered by a blanket, a shape that moved slightly and was unmistakably human. She pushed at the door and it swung open with a creak.

She said, 'Is something wrong? Can I help you?' And as she moved towards the bed, the figure stirred and the covering blanket fell away slightly revealing a tousled blond head. Rachel knew one minute's overpowering relief that it wasn't Vitas, and then her heart nearly stopped as she gazed down at the haggard face staring up at her, the eyes widening in utter incredulity, muffled sounds coming from behind the dirty gag which had been stuffed into his mouth.

It was Mark.

She gave a little gasp and fell on her knees beside the bed, tearing at the gag to free it.

'Rachie,' he choked, 'it's you! I thought I was seeing things! What are you doing here? How did you know where I was?'

'It's a long story.' She saw with horror how thin he was and that there was a feverish spot on each of his cheeks. He looked ill and hungry. 'But what happened? How did you get like this?'

He moved impatiently. 'There's no time to talk. You've got to get out of here—get help.'

'I'm going nowhere without you,' she said. 'I'll help you up.'

He threw back the blanket. 'I can't get up.'

She looked down and saw that his right leg was chained to the bed, the chain fastened by a hefty padlock.

'Who did this?' she demanded hoarsely.

'I don't know.' He closed his eyes wearily. 'They arrived about a fortnight ago. I'd been poking around in some of the old mine-workings, but I hadn't found anything. They were bloody dangerous as well. I felt if I took too deep a breath the whole damned lot would cave in on me. I was just going to give it up as a bad job and go back to Bogota when—they came. When I came back here and found them, I didn't worry too much at first. I'd been camping out here and there was plenty of room for all of us—or that's what I thought. Then they started asking questions about what I'd been doing I didn't see why I had to reply. I mean—I knew damned well that what I'd been doing wasn't within the strict letter of the law; the Colombian government doesn't exactly approve of people wandering about helping themselves to their emeralds. But they seemed to think I knew something that they wanted to know. They went through my stuff and when I argued, one of them hit me. I woke up in here—like this.'

'Oh, my God!' Rachel gasped numbly.

The hoarse voice went on. 'They said at first that I wouldn't eat again until I told them what they wanted to know, but after a couple of days it seemed to dawn on them that I didn't know anything. I gather they'd been poking around in the old workings themselves and seen how poor the pickings were. Then the man who seemed to be the leader came to see me. He said they were going to let me go. I was so relieved, I nearly burst into tears. But he said I had to write a letter first. I thought it was going to be a kind of statement exonerating them in case I decided to complain to the authorities when I got away from this accursed place. But it wasn't, of course. The letter was to Grandfather and it was a ransom note.'

'Ransom?' She stared at him in horror. 'Mark, you haven't! That's why I'm here. Grandfather has been very ill—it's his heart. He was really afraid this time—that's why he asked me to come and find you.'

'But how did he know where I was?' Mark passed the arm of a filthy shirt wearily across his eyes.

'A friend saw you dining out in Bogota. You were with the Arviles family.'

'Oh, yes.' He produced a parody of his usual smile. 'It was Isabel's birthday. God, it seems a lifetime ago—a different world. Rachel.' His other hand groped for hers and held it. His fingers were cold and clammy. 'I—I didn't know that things like this happened—for real.'

She gave a little shudder, remembering the photographs in Maria's box—the proud father, and the laughing boy with his dark, sparkling eyes ...

'You don't know the half of it,' she said. 'Did—did you write that note?'

He shook his head.

'Thank God!' She squeezed his hand. 'It would kill Grandfather.'

'If I don't write it, it's going to kill me.' His voice was almost unemotional. 'They've given me until tomorrow to do as they want. That's why you've got to get out, go and find someone. Even in this forgotten corner, there's got to be some form of law and order somewhere.'

His voice rose almost desperately.

Rachel said, 'It's all right. There's the man who brought me here. He'll know what to do.'

'Where is he?' He peered past her.

A fair point. Her heart sank within her as she said, 'Well, I'm not too sure, right now, but ...'

'How do you know he isn't one of them?' he said, and the hopeless note in his voice chilled her.

The simple answer was, 'Because I love him, and I couldn't love anyone capable of doing this to another human being.' But she didn't attempt to give it. Instead she bent and brushed her lips across his hot forehead.

'I'll go now,' she said. 'Stall them. Promise anything you have to ...' She stopped, because Mark's face was changing. He looked very young and very pinched, and he was staring over her shoulder.

The man filling the narrow doorway said, 'Another little bird in my net. This time a pretty hen.'

There was something about the way he said it that made her shrivel inside. She went on holding Mark's hand and looking at the newcomer. He could have been any age, thick-set with grizzled hair and a heavy moustache.

He was carrying a crude lamp in his hand and he set it down on a broken chair before he walked over to Rachel, taking her chin in his hand, and studying her face from various angles.

'A very pretty hen. And from the same brood as our young cockerel here.' He chuckled suddenly. 'Now why, I ask myself? How did you get here, *chiquita*, and what do you want?'

'I came here alone,' she said. 'And I came to fetch my brother.'

He chuckled again. '*Bravo*, I like your spirit, little one. Perhaps you should have been the man. Yet you must not lie to me. Who came here with you?' His fingers tightened until she thought that he meant to break her jaw. She wanted to cry out against the pain, and she sank her teeth into her lip trying to fight one agony with another.

Another voice said, 'I know how she came here, *señor*. I can tell you everything.'

It was a voice Rachel recognised, and she could understand the note of malicious triumph it held as well.

Her tormentor released her. He said gently, 'Speak then, Arnaldez, little worm.'

Carlos' eyes sparked dislike at her from the doorway. He said, 'This is the *Inglesa* I told you of, Señor Rodriguez. She is the woman of Vitas de Mendoza.'

Rodriguez. Rachel felt herself sway slightly on her feet.

She heard him laugh. He said almost amiably, 'Sit down, *chiquita.* We must take special care of Mendoza's woman. And how is the young lord of the Llanos? He has been a nuisance to me lately with this crazy thirst for revenge of his. He seems to blame me for some misfortunes his family suffered years ago, and the army have been making my life difficult ever since. I have been wanting to talk to him about it, and now my chance has come. Where is he, little one?'

Rachel said, white-lipped, 'He's not here. We—we quarrelled. He left me.'

Rodriguez looked at her for a long time without speaking. Then he sighed deeply and shook his head.

'You do not tell me the truth, *señorita,* and I do not like that. If I were an ill-tempered man, I would punish you, as I punished your handsome lover all those years ago.' He saw her flinch, and smiled. 'But we will not speak of such things. And you must not hate me for spoiling his good looks, *chiquita.* At least I did not spoil him in the way that matters most to a woman.'

He saw the colour storm into her face and a silent chuckle shook him. Beside her she felt Mark stir restlessly. Carlos, she was thankful to see, had vanished.

Rodriguez went on, 'Presently we will all go out into the courtyard and we will build a fire and bring lights, and we will invite your lover to join us.'

Rachel said numbly, 'You're wasting your time. He won't come.'

He ran an almost caressing finger down one of her loosened strands of blonde hair.

'I think he will, little one. I think he will. In his place, I would come running.'

He went out, dragging the door closed behind him, and Rachel sank down on the edge of the bed again.

Mark demanded, 'And what was that all about? Who is this Vitas de Mendoza?'

She did not look at him. 'The man who brought me here. The one I was telling you about.'

He gave an angry laugh. 'You forgot to tell me you were his mistress.'

Rachel said wearily, 'I didn't forget—and I'm not. And since when have you been the arbiter of my morals anyway?'

'I'm sorry,' he said stiffly.

'Don't be.' She stared at one dusty boot. 'At one time I was counting on your protection from him.' She smiled bitterly. 'That also seems a lifetime ago.'

'If you ask me all these Latins are the same,' he said broodingly. 'They're hardly allowed to touch their own girls before the marriage ceremony. Miguel was telling me that someone was receiving a prize from a beauty queen once and he kissed her on the cheek, and her outraged father nearly lynched him. It's no wonder they think tourists fair game.'

'This,' she said grittily, 'is hardly the conversation we need to be having at this moment.'

'No,' he said soberly. He shot her a look. 'This Mendoza —will he help us?'

'I don't know.' She spread her hands helplessly. 'For one thing, he doesn't know where I am. He told me to stay where I was and wait for him.'

'It's a pity you didn't,' he said morosely. 'Oh, I'm sorry, Rachie. But you can't escape the fact we're in one hell of a mess. And part of it could have been avoided if you'd done as you were told.'

'Yes,' she said almost inaudibly. 'Yes—I know that.' She bowed her head and began to cry, great gulping sobs that tore at her chest and throat.

'Rachel, love!' Mark pulled himself into an awkward sitting position and put his arms round her. 'Oh, God I didn't mean it. What did I say?'

'Nothing,' she said desolately. 'It's all right. Just leave me alone.'

He said helplessly, 'Oh, lord! It's this man, isn't it? This Mendoza. How long have you known him?'

'I don't know.' She blew her nose fiercely on a bedraggled handkerchief, 'But you may as well know you can count it in hours as well as days.'

He said nothing, but she could sense his dismay, and, in a way, understand it. It was so out of character. Mark knew she had always played it cool in her relationships with men.

He said at last, 'He must be quite something. I'm looking forward to meeting him.'

She said fiercely, 'I hope you don't. I hope he rides away from this place and keeps going. You heard Rodriguez. He can't wait to get his hands on him again—because years ago he killed his father and disfigured Vitas for life, and now he wants to complete what he started, with some additional refinements, no doubt.'

'And what about us?' Mark sounded almost sullen. 'The outlook is none too healthy for us, quite apart from your Colombian Romeo. I suppose this—Rodriguez may insist we go on with the ransom demand.'

'But we can't,' she protested. 'I told you Grandfather has been very ill. To get such a demand would be the death of him.'

'And I suppose to have the pair of us simply vanish off the face of the earth will do him all the good in the world,' he snapped. Then a look of contrition came over his face. 'Oh, love, I'm sorry. I don't know what I'm saying half the time. This past two weeks, all I've had to do is lie here on this damned bed and be frightened out of my wits. I'm not thinking straight any more.'

'I know,' she said gently. 'Mark, was it the Flame of Diablo you came to find?'

He flushed. 'Yes, if you must know. There are so many stories about it, I thought it couldn't possibly be all myth.' His voice hushed. 'Can you imagine, Rachel, a fortune contained in one green stone you could carry in the palm of your hand?'

'Yes, I can quite imagine. Oh, God, I wish Miguel
Arviles had kept his mouth shut! Mark, can't you see—if
it ever existed at all, it will have been found years ago. It's
probably part of—a hundred engagement rings by now.
Besides, isn't it also part of the story that the Flame of
Diablo has a curse on it?'

'Oh, that,' he shrugged. 'That's just superstition.'

'Is it?' she asked drily. 'Are things going so wonderfully
well in your life just at the moment?'

'Don't be daft,' he muttered defensively. 'I didn't catch
a glimpse of any emeralds, large or small.'

'No, but you went looking, and perhaps for the old gods,
that's enough,' she said quietly.

He looked beyond her to the door. 'I see they've got
their fire started,' he commented, clearly glad to change
the subject.

Rachel swung round and looked at the flickering light
which illumined the grating. The door swung open and
Rodriguez looked in.

'It is time, *chiquita*,' he observed almost jovially. He
stood back and two of his men came in. One of them unlocked the padlock and removed the chain from Mark's leg,
and the other pulled him to his feet. He could hardly stand
and he cried out in pain as they tried to march him to the
door.

Rachel swung round to Rodriguez, a protest quivering on
her lips. But she did not utter it. As their eyes met, she
seemed to see him properly for the first time—a soulless
predator who was quite indifferent to the suffering of
others, and she had no wish to amuse him by embarking on
useless pleas for mercy. Her head high, she followed Mark
out into the courtyard.

The bonfire they had lit illumined every corner. Even
the big gate had been dragged off what remained of its
hinges and piled on top. As she looked round, Rachel
realised that Rodriguez' gang only consisted of half a dozen
men, but they were all armed. Carlos was there, skulking
in a corner, and she guessed he was not officially part of the
gang. Perhaps an informer that they used from time to

time, she thought with contempt, remembering the eager voice volunteering the fatal news.

Rodriguez took up his stance in the middle of the courtyard.

'Vitas!' he bellowed. 'Vitas de Mendoza!' His voice seemed to echo and re-echo in the stillness of the night. 'We have your pretty one, *amigo*. If you wish to see her once again as she was the last time you held her in your arms, then come down to us now.'

Only the silence answered him, a long and terrible blank. Rachel's hands twisted together until the knuckles whitened. A soundless prayer repeated over and over again in her mind. Don't let him come. Please don't let him come.

'Vitas!' Rodriguez shouted again, and she could see in the firelight the muscle jumping in his face which meant he was angry. 'This is your last chance, and the last chance of your *enamorador*. I count to ten, and then I give her to my men to play with.'

'Don't shout, Rodriguez.' He was suddenly standing just outside the circle of firelight, his hat tipped over his face. 'I may be half blind, thanks to your good offices, but I am by no means deaf.'

Rachel whispered imploringly, 'Vitas—no!' But perhaps she only uttered the words in her heart, because he did not even give her a glance as he stepped forward.

'So we meet again, *amigo*.' Rodriguez' chest rose and fell as he studied the tall lean figure standing composedly before him.

'A meeting I have long desired,' Vitas said courteously.

Rodriguez began to shake with laughter. 'But not quite in these circumstances, eh? You had other ideas. Other notions.' He spat contemptuously. 'You are not the first, and you will not be the last.'

Vitas spoke softly. 'So—you have me. And that is what you wanted. But the woman—and the man—you don't want them, Rodriguez. You don't need them.'

Rodriguez' smile widened. 'No, *amigo*? Perhaps it is true. Perhaps I will let them go—but only to the highest bidder, you understand.' He sniggered. 'Carlos Arnaldez has a fancy for the girl. Can you offer a higher price?'

Vitas said evenly, 'Perhaps. What do you want?'

Rodriguez pretended to consider. His glee was horrible, Rachel thought with a weird detachment.

'What can I ask from the young lord of the Llanos?' he pondered. 'His private plane to fly me wherever I wish to go? One of his vast herds of cattle? Ten million *pesos*?'

Vitas stood waiting, his hands resting lightly on his narrow hips.

'But no,' Rodriguez slapped his thigh as if a thought had suddenly come to him. 'I'll ask for something I asked another member of your family for a long time ago. Perhaps you will be more amenable.' His eyes were suddenly fierce. 'Give me the map,' he said. 'The map which shows where the Flame of Diablo can be found.'

Beside her, Rachel heard Mark gasp loudly in excitement. Her face burned as Vitas turned slowly to look at them. His gaze was cynical and contemptuous as it travelled over her, then, as it reached the fair-haired boy at her side, she saw him stiffen slightly. He had just assimilated the twin facts that Mark was not only younger than she was, but also a blood relation, she thought guiltily.

Vitas turned back to Rodriguez. 'There is no map,' he said flatly. 'The secret of the Diablo mine has been passed down from father to son for generations in my family without a line being drawn or a word being written. That has been its safeguard.'

'Safeguard!' Rodriguez sneered. 'What safeguard was there from your grasping ancestors?'

Vitas said laconically, 'No one from my family has ever benefited from the Diablo mine. We recognised early in our history that the mine was a sacred place to the old gods. Only my great-grandfather did not want to believe that and he gave the money for the foundation of this mission'—his lips twisted—'to Christianise the valley, and drive the old gods out.' He shrugged. 'You see for yourself what success he met with.'

'Stories to frighten children,' Rodriguez muttered. 'But I am not frightened, and tomorrow you will show me where the Diablo mine is to be found. That is the price I ask in order to let the *Inglesa* go.'

'Both the girl—and her brother.' Only Rachel caught the slight stress which Vitas placed on the last word.

Rodriguez waved his hands impatiently. 'Both—both. But——' his fleshy lips stretched in a fixed smile, 'you *amigo*, I shall not let go. I should have killed you years ago, but instead I decided to be merciful. It is always a mistake, and you have caused me many problems.' His voice thickened. 'But after tomorrow, you will be no problem at all.'

Vitas' whole attention seemed to be concentrated on lighting one of his cigars. 'As you say,' he observed noncommittally when the task was completed to his satisfaction.

'Take him away.' Rodriguez gestured, and two of his men stepped forward. 'Put him in the room at the end. And no need to tie him up,' he added, grinning. 'If he runs away in the night, he knows well what will happen to his woman in the morning.'

Rachel watched them take him. He did not even spare Mark or herself a glance as he went by. She swallowed. She had tricked him and disastrously disobeyed him in the space of twenty-four hours, and yet to save her, he was giving up a cherished family secret, and ultimately, unless a miracle occurred, his own life.

'And tuck our two little pigeons up for the night,' Rodriguez directed. 'Put the girl in the cell next to her brother.' They can knock on the wall to each other,' he added with a chuckle.

She walked past the man who tried to take her arm and approached Rodriguez. She said, 'I want to ask you a favour.'

'Ask on, *chiquita*.' His tone was bland, but there was suspicion in the hard dark eyes.

'You said that being merciful was a mistake,' she said steadily. 'Well, I want you to make one more mistake. Please don't shut me up in a cell on my own. Let me spend this last night with Señor de Mendoza.'

For a moment he stared at her incredulously, and then

he began to laugh. 'I like you, *Inglesa*,' he choked. 'A night for the lord of the Llanos to remember, eh, before all memories cease for him. Go to him, *chica*, and tell him he has Rodriguez to thank for this.'

The leer of the guard followed her into the room. The door swung to behind her, and she heard the thud as the heavy bar which secured it dropped into place. Then there was silence.

CHAPTER NINE

THE room was not completely dark. A small lamp, consisting of a dish of some kind of grease with a cotton wick floating in it, stood on a chair near the narrow bed.

Vitas was stretched full-length on the bed, his hands linked at the back of his neck. Rachel stood and looked at him, remembering with a pang how short a time it was since she had entered that hotel room in Asuncion and found him lying on her bed waiting for her. Then, she had been able to fight the physical attraction she felt for him with fear and mistrust, and since that time she had forged herself other weapons to use against him. But tonight she was defenceless.

Slowly he turned his head and looked at her.

'What do you want?' he asked flatly.

She moistened her lips with the tip of her tongue. She hadn't expected him to leap up and seize her in his arms after all that had happened, but she had expected more encouragement than that.

'I've come to—be with you. Rodriguez said I must tell you that you have him to thank.'

'Rodriguez can go to the hell that is surely waiting for him,' he said savagely. 'And you may go with him. And take your pity with you.'

'I'm not here out of pity,' she protested.

'Your gratitude, then. You are transparent, Raquel, do

you know that? You imagine I am about to gallantly make the supreme sacrifice for you so you romantically decide to do the same for me. Well, you may sacrifice your precious virginity elsewhere. Why not with your *novio*?' he added sneeringly. 'Your eager lover who looks as if he's never laid a hand on a woman in passion in his life.'

'Don't be ridiculous!' Unshed tears were hurting her throat. 'You know perfectly well that I just made that story up, and that Mark's my brother.'

'I know perfectly well what was about to happen between us when you decided to surprise me with your little invention,' he threw at her harshly. 'Do you know what happens to a man when the girl in his arms goes with him to the point of surrender, and then changes her mind? Agony, *querida*, not merely emotional but physical. Well, I don't propose to spend my last night on earth twisted into knots because you draw back at the last minute once again.'

'But it won't be like that.' Her hands twisted together. 'Oh, what can I say to convince you?'

He lifted a shoulder. 'I can't imagine why you should want to convince me. You've been fighting me since our first meeting, so this sudden capitulation has an interest, I suppose. What has kindled this passion in you, *chicá*? Rodriguez' revelation that I'm a millionaire? Are you hoping for a mention in my will—for services rendered?'

'That's cruel,' she muttered, her voice shaking.

'I'm not feeling particularly kind.' He gave her a sombre look. 'You're getting off lightly, *chica*. Last night, I promised I would be gentle with you. Tonight I'd guarantee nothing. Now knock on the door and tell the guard that this time I've changed my mind.'

'I shall do nothing of the sort!' There was an empty box piled up with some other lumber in a corner of the room, and Rachel dragged it forward and sat on it. She said, 'Please don't send me away, Vitas. I—I don't want to be on my own tonight.' She waited desperately, but he did not reply. She went on in a low voice, 'Why—why don't you want me to stay? Don't you—want me any more?'

'Want you?' He rolled over suddenly on his side, his

dark face blazing with anger as he looked at her. '*Dios*, you little fool, don't you understand anything? Of course I want you. I've wanted you ever since I saw you standing in the doorway at Ramirez' place. Haven't I made it clear to you—with every word, every look, every touch?'

'Then why...?' she could not complete the sentence, just held out her hands in mute appeal.

'Do I really have to spell it out to you?' He swung his long legs to the floor and sat gripping the edge of the thin mattress so tightly that his knuckles were white with the strain. 'Because for one thing, Raquel, I wish to send you back to England without too many memories—or too many regrets.'

'Do you think I'm going to find you as easy to forget as that?' she demanded raggedly.

'Everything passes in time, *querida*. But if I took you, you could well have an all too potent reminder of my brief intrusion into your life—you could find you were carrying my child.' A faint smile touched his lips as he saw her flush slightly. 'Something which had not occurred to you?'

'No,' she admitted. 'But if that's your only reason——'

'It isn't.' His voice was almost laconic. 'To be frank, *querida*, I am scarcely in the mood for a lengthy seduction, as I hinted just now. Tonight my needs would be better served by a woman of the streets rather than an inexperienced girl. Do I make myself clear?'

'Brutally clear.' Rachel lifted her chin. 'But are your needs the only ones to be considered? You are assuming that Rodriguez will keep his side of the bargain tomorrow and let Mark and me go, but you can't guarantee it.'

'That's only too true,' he said coolly. 'But I hoped you wouldn't think about it too closely. So what are you suggesting? That we should try and forget in each other's arms that dawn waits beneath the horizon?' He smiled. 'That isn't very realistic.'

'Perhaps not,' she said. 'But then none of this seems very real. It's like one of those nightmares that you know is only a dream but yet can't wake from.'

'Like the one you experienced last night?'

'Yes,' she said. 'Which you woke me from. Wake me again, Vitas. *Por favor.*'

He groaned. '*Dios*, Raquel, you tempt me. Do you know how much?'

'Not enough, obviously.' She stood up, pushing back the box. 'Shall I strip for you?' Her hands went to the buttons of her shirt. 'I shared a dressing room last year with a girl who'd worked as a stripper when she couldn't find anything else. She showed me some of the tricks one evening, for a giggle. I've no music, and I'm wearing the wrong gear, but it might amuse you ...'

'It would not amuse me in the slightest,' he said icily. Two long strides brought him to her, pulling her bruisingly into his arms. 'And you may forget what tricks she taught you. I don't need that kind of stimulation, *querida*. I need the sight, the scent, the feel of you.' His voice thickened and broke off as his mouth claimed hers with ruthless passion. Rachel clung to him without reserve, her lips parting willingly under the insistent pressure of his. Without taking his mouth from hers, he lifted her into his arms and carried her back to the bed.

She had offered herself, and she had expected to be taken, even used. She was prepared and willing for that—anything that would keep the darkness from him, and her generosity reaped its own overwhelming rewards. His initiation of her was almost wickedly controlled yet passionate, consummately skilful, but tender. Her first inevitable shyness dissolved away in his arms, as he taught her to respond, to return the pleasure she received, a pleasure that superseded and transcended the first sharp pain of possession.

When it was over, she lay trembling in the aftermath of a delight she had never dreamed of knowing, and there were tears on her face, tears of joy, gratitude and disbelief. And Vitas kissed the tears away and murmured to her in Spanish, every word a caress. She fell asleep, her fair head pillowed against his chest, her slim body totally relaxed against his, and later he woke her with a trail of light teasing kisses across her throat and breasts, until, at last, his mouth was teasing no longer but burning her with a fire that threatened to consume her utterly. She could only cling to him and allow herself to be swept away on the force of his passion, dying a little death in his arms.

Some time later she opened her eyes and realised that she was alone. She sat up, noticing in alarm that there was a pale light emanating from the tiny square window high in the wall.

'*Si*,' Vitas said quietly. 'It is dawn, *querida*.'

She saw that he had re-lit the lamp and was using the box as a writing table.

'What are you writing?' she asked bewilderedly.

'A letter to my mother.' He sealed the envelope.

'But where did you get the paper and the pen?'

'I imagine they were originally the property of your brother,' he said. 'I asked one of Rodriguez' men to get them for me last night.'

He came back to the bed and lay down beside her. 'I have something to give you, *amada*.'

She tried to smile, but made a mess of it. 'There—there has to be a joke in that line.'

'Perhaps.' He leaned forward and kissed her mouth lingeringly. 'And presently we will both enjoy—the joke. But first we must talk. *Chica*, neither you nor I know what the day will bring to us, but let us assume that Rodriguez will keep his word and let you and your brother leave Diablo as agreed. The horses are tied up near to where I left you last night. Ride as far and as fast as you can. As soon as you reach an army post, stop and tell them what has happened, and say to them that I request they escort you to my house near Villavicencio. Do you understand?'

'Yes.' Her eyes widened endlessly as she looked at him. 'But why to your house, Vitas?'

'Because I hope you will take my letter to my mother,' he said quietly. He unfastened the medallion he wore and put it round her neck, allowing the silver chain to slip into place in the valley between her breasts.

'One last thing,' he added. 'I will try and persuade Rodriguez to let you go before I show him the mine. But if he refuses, there could be danger for you, *querida*, so you must promise to obey me instantly if I give you an order. If I say "Run" then you run at once. If I say "Get down", then you fall to the ground immediately. And your brother too.'

'Vitas——' she began chokingly.

'No more talk.' He leaned forward and kissed the smooth hollow where the medallion lay. 'Remember what I have said. And don't cry, *mi amada*, for we are not beaten yet. Life is still sweet—and soon will be sweeter.'

Rachel was calm and dressed when the door was unbarred. Vitas' letter was tucked down inside her boot, and the medallion lay, a cool and unfamiliar weight, between her breasts, her shirt buttoned high to conceal it.

She walked past the guard, her head held high, and out into the sunshine. The first person she saw was Mark. He was standing by the dead bonfire, staring down at the blackened embers. He had a tin mug in his hand. After a moment's hesitation, she walked across and joined him, slipping her hand through his arm.

'They didn't chain you up last night?'

'No.' His manner was peculiar to say the least. He didn't look at her, and his face wore an odd expression between hostility and embarrassment.

She persevered, 'Is that coffee you've got? I'd love some.'

'It's filthy stuff,' he muttered. Then, giving her a sharp sideways glance, 'Didn't the condemned man invite you to share his hearty breakfast? From the lewd jokes that have been passed around this morning, I gather you've shared everything else with him.'

Rachel felt as if he had struck her in the face.

'Yes, I slept with Vitas last night. Does it matter?'

'Matter?' His voice was outraged. 'God, isn't everything bad enough without you—degrading yourself with one of the top Colombian studs, for a bunch of greasy cut-throats to snigger over?'

Her face was white. 'How dare you!'

'How dared you?' he retorted. 'You know what this

would do to Grandfather if he ever found out.'

She said tonelessly, 'The only way he'll find out is if you tell him. And remember we still have to get back to England first.'

Mark looked down scowling. 'I haven't forgotten,' he muttered.

She said with difficulty, 'Mark love, we shouldn't quarrel. Not at a time like this.'

He said defensively, 'I know, Rachie. But if you'd only heard what they've been saying—especially that little creep they call Carlos—and in English, to make sure I understood.'

'It must have been most upsetting for you.' Her tone was ironic. 'Perhaps it's slipped your mind that Vitas has bartered a family secret that his father died for in order to save us?'

'He hasn't saved us yet.' Mark's tone was still sullen, but she could hear the fear behind it, and forgave him in a flood of protective feeling. He was spoiled, and she had always known that, because he had been the wanted boy. No one had ever denied him anything and in her way she had been his devoted slave almost as much as their grandfather. Now, suddenly, he was way out of his depth, ill and frightened and striking out at everyone around him.

'But he will,' she said gently. She meant it to be a reassurance, but even as she spoke, the thought came to her that even so, Vitas might not be able to save himself, and her eyes were filled with the brilliance of tears.

Mark muttered furiously, 'My God!' Then he threw the remains of his coffee away on the charred debris of the fire and stalked away.

'In there?' Rodriguez demanded incredulously. He was sweating profusely in the intense heat, and Rachel, standing just to one side of him could see that dangerous little muscle leaping in his face. 'You think to make a fool of me —Rodriguez?' He gestured towards the dark creeper-clad opening. 'We have searched in there. It is empty, except for bats and snakes.'

'You doubt my word?' There was an unmistakable challenge in Vitas' voice. 'We made a bargain. The Flame of Diablo burns in that cave. Reach out, little man, and take it.'

He was mocking, deliberately provocative, and Rachel's heart thumped in alarm. She could sense Mark's unease. His arm was trembling against hers, just above the cord which bound their wrists together.

Rachel felt a drop of sweat running down her forehead, she lifted her free hand and wiped it away. Everything seemed to be going wrong. Rodriguez had refused point blank to let Mark and herself go. They were his hostages, he said, and they would not be released until he held the Flame in his hand. She had half expected Vitas to protest, but he had shrugged, and walked over to where she stood, her wrist already roped to Mark's.

'It is time to say *adios, querida*.' He sounded casual to the point of insolence. 'Remember me.' Without haste he bent and kissed her on the mouth, a long and sensuous kiss which left her trembling and weak. As he released her, 'Remember,' he repeated, then walked away.

Beside her, she heard Mark mutter 'Bastard!' but she knew, as he could not that Vitas was not asking her to remember him as a lover, but to recall to mind the orders he had given her and act on them. She wished she could explain, but with Rodriguez' men all round them it was impossible.

She had walked tensely at Mark's side as they made their way out of the old mission and down the valley.

Even before Rodriguez' outburst, she had heard Mark draw a sharp breath and whisper, 'What the hell's he playing at? There's nothing here, Rachie. I've combed every inch of those tunnels.'

For the first time Rodriguez looked indecisive, less than in full control of the situation. Behind her, Rachel could hear his men growing restive, murmuring among themselves.

'What is the matter, Rodriguez?' Vitas taunted again. 'Are you afraid that the Flame may scorch, after all?'

'Don't talk to me of fear,' Rodriguez muttered hoarsely. 'When I have finished with you, you will know it well. You will crawl to me begging for death.'

Rachel felt a quiver of fear and revulsion run through her body at the gloating words, but Vitas seemed entirely unmoved, even faintly amused.

'And now the other part of the bargain,' he said softly. 'The girl and her brother. Let them go.'

Again she could sense the hesitation in Rodriguez. There was something animal in his eyes as he turned and looked at Rachel and Mark, before swinging back to Vitas, who stood waiting, his hands on his hips, his whole attitude one of cool indifference.

'No,' he said menacingly. 'Not now. Not yet. I don't trust you, my fine *señor*. They will go with us into the tunnel to answer for your good faith—and your good behaviour. One false move from you and I shoot your woman in the stomach.'

'Then at least untie them. The tunnel is narrow in places, and low in others. They will never manage it roped together —unless you wish to wait while they crawl after us on their knees,' he added with a faint shrug.

For a moment Rodriguez glared at him suspiciously, but he gave the necessary order, and Rachel winced as the cord fell away and the blood began to flow back into her numbed hand. She rubbed the chafed flesh with her fingers and as she did so was suddenly aware that Vitas was looking at her. He turned away at once, but in that brief second she had seen in his face such a deadly murderous rage that the breath caught in her throat.

She glanced at Mark to see if he had noticed anything, but he was attending to his own aches and pains. He looked very young and very pale. She touched his arm, aware that Rodriguez and Vitas were approaching the mouth of the tunnel and that the other men were watching them.

'Do exactly as you're told,' she whispered. 'Whatever Vitas says and as soon as he says it.'

He gave her a furious look. 'I'm not his damned puppet!'

She couldn't argue with him because they too were being urged forward towards the tunnel entrance. She bent her head to enter, feeling the creepers brush against her skin like cold green fingers.

It was damp in the tunnel, a chill dank smell, like the inside of a tomb. She shivered, wishing the analogy had not occurred to her.

'This is bloody dangerous,' Mark muttered close to her ear, as if he had picked up her thoughts. 'One wrong move —one loud noise even and the whole lot could come crashing in on us. I hope that arrogant swine knows what he's doing.'

As if to emphasise his words, some stones and dust fell from the roof just ahead of them and clattered to the floor. Rachel's foot touched something solid and she looked down startled to see the broken, decaying remains of a pickaxe. Simply discarded, she wondered, or thrown down in terror as its user fled—from what?

The darkness closed inexorably around them as they penetrated more deeply into the tunnel. Rodriguez was carrying a powerful torch, as was one of the two men accompanying them, and the beams of light roamed endlessly over the crumbling walls, searching for the tell-tale green veins.

Rachel realised that it was becoming more difficult to breathe. Was it merely unsuspected claustrophobia, she wondered, or was there no fresh air? She put a hand apprehensively to her throat.

'Where are the emeralds?' Rodriguez snarled, the torch beam wavering crazily as he turned on Vitas. 'Dog and son of a dog, you have lied to me!'

'Keep your voice down,' Vitas said quietly, 'or your next angry word could be your last.'

'Faugh! There's no air in this hole.' Rodriguez' hand tugged at the neck of his shirt.

'Then why waste what there is in discussing it?' Vitas was cool and unruffled. 'Are you prepared to go on?'

'Go on where?' Rodriguez growled suspiciously. 'The tunnel comes to a dead end. I tell you I have combed every inch of it.'

'Not every inch, or even every yard,' Vitas returned. 'You're a creature of earth, Rodriguez. A man must lift his eyes if he wishes to find the gods.'

The torchlight swept upwards and Rachel suppressed a gasp as she saw the narrow black gap above their heads.

'Up there?' Rodriguez sounded incredulous, and Rachel could not blame him. The opening in the rock looked hardly wide enough to admit a child, let alone a full-grown man.

'Up there,' Vitas agreed mockingly.

'Then you first. And after you the girl.'

Rachel stood watching disbelievingly as Vitas reached up and caught at the edge of the rock, levering himself up into the gap. Rodriguez made an impatient gesture with his gun and she stepped forward. Mark lifted her and from the darkness, Vitas bent to grip her wrists and draw her up beside him.

There was no torchlight here, but the darkness seemed full of a strange glow. She blinked, turning her head, and Vitas' hand came over her mouth stifling her involuntary cry.

The golden skull sat on its dusty ledge as it had done for centuries, the great emeralds which filled the empty eye sockets seeming to glare with a life of their own at these intruders into its sacred solitude.

The stones in the eyes had been cut and polished, but there were other emeralds in the cave still in their natural state, as they had been cut from the earth, and heaped in offering to the gods.

Vitas' arms went round her, lifting her again. 'Up you go, *querida*. As fast as you can.'

She was in another tunnel which seemed to have been carved through the solid rock, a tunnel where there was only room to lie flat and wriggle forward, clawing her way upwards using her nails and her toes as leverage. But there was air somewhere ahead of her. Its freshness was in her nostrils, on her tongue, and she gasped for it, lifting her face gratefully, stretching out her arms, as if, absurdly, she could touch it.

She felt her wrists grabbed, and someone was dragging

her forwards, hurting her as her slim body grazed itself on
the rock, but it didn't matter because there was sun on her
face after the suffocating darkness.

She looked up dazedly into a bronzed face, shaded by a
smart uniform cap. A handsome face with a small black
moustache.

'Señorita. I regret that I had to be so rough.' He helped
her to her feet. 'I am Captain Lopez—Vitas may have mentioned me.'

'No.' Her hands were bleeding a little and her nails were
ruined. She knew the spectacle she must make, covered in
earth, a rip in her shirt and another in the leg of her jeans.
Captain Lopez, as if sensing her discomfort, made a quick
signal and a soldier stepped forward proffering a uniform
jacket for her to put round her shoulders. Someone else was
holding out a cigarette case, and now, as she looked round,
she could see that the clifftop seemed to be alive with uni-
formed men.

'What's going on?' She turned desperately to Captain
Lopez, but he made a sharp gesture, bidding her to be
quiet. His whole attitude was tense and listening, and instinctively Rachel tensed too, straining her own ears.

The sound of the shot when it came was unmistakable,
muffled though it was, and equally unmistakable was the
rumble which followed it, rising to a roar.

She heard Captain Lopez whisper a blasphemy and saw
him plunging away from her. The muffled roar went on
and on as if tons of rocks and earth were flooding the fragile
passages beneath her feet, and she fell down on to the earth,
her fingers tearing at the grass which covered it, crying his
name, as if she would dig with her bare hands to reach the
man she loved. Thin choking dust was ascending from the
tunnel she had just used, invading her mouth, making her
eyes stream.

She said, 'Vitas,' over and over again like a desperate
litany, her imagination creating for her the terrible picture
of the lithe bronze body which she had clasped in ecstasy
lying crushed and broken in the darkness below.

She was crying in earnest now, the tears pouring from

her smarting eyes and making runnels in the grime on her face. She pressed her fist against her mouth like a child, trying to suppress the moans which rose up inside her.

Hands touched her, and she stiffened in rejection. 'Leave me. Go away,' she begged. 'I just want to die!'

'But life is still sweet, *querida*, as I told you last night.'

She rolled over on to her back, her eyes widening with disbelief as she stared up at him. He was as dirty as she was, his clothes in shreds. There was a nasty contusion on his forehead, and blood welling from a gash on his shoulder, clearly visible through his torn shirt.

'Vitas!' She flung herself into his arms which closed round her, crushing her against him. 'What happened? How did you get out?'

'The same way as you did, Raquel, but without Pablo's helping hands to assist me over the last few yards.' His mouth claimed hers with hungry possessiveness. 'At one point I didn't think I was going to make it, then I heard you calling me, *amada*, *queridissima*.'

'I thought you were dead. I heard the shot—and then the landslip begin. I didn't see how anyone could survive down there ...' She broke off and stared at him, suddenly numb with horror. 'Mark,' she whispered. 'Oh God—how could I have forgotten? Where is he? You didn't bring him with you.'

'He was still in the lower tunnel when I provoked Rodriguez into firing his gun. I told him to run. If he obeyed, then he has a chance.' He took her in his arms again, stroking her hair. 'I would have got him out with you through the air shaft, *querida*, if it had been possible. You know that.'

'Yes,' she said dully. She turned her face into his uninjured shoulder and stayed still and quiet, resting against him, trying to regain her control.

After a while, Vitas helped her to her feet, and they began the slow difficult descent to the base of the cliff. She could see the remaining members of Rodriguez' gang, including Carlos, being rounded up by the military and herded away at gun-point. But she couldn't even rejoice in that. Her eyes were drawn painfully to the tunnel entrance where soldiers were digging. She remembered the dream she'd had, and began to tremble.

'Vitas, *amigo*.' Captain Lopez approached at a run. '*Por Dios*, I would not have believed anyone could survive such an earthquake.' He gestured behind him. 'They are bringing them out now.'

Rachel made a small convulsive movement and his eyes went to her.

'Oh, not your brother, *señorita*. He has a broken leg, but he is alive. He was almost at the entrance when the rockfall began. One of my men is putting a splint on his leg, and then you may talk to him—reassure yourself.'

'Captain Lopez,' Rachel's voice shook, 'I'm going to kiss you.'

'*Señorita*.' The look he sent Vitas was wary in the extreme, but his smile was delighted. 'I should be honoured.'

He bent his head while she pressed her lips to his cheek.

'All my life,' she said, 'I shall remember you pulling me out of that hole into the air. It was a miracle, your being there like that. And now you've given Mark back to me.'

He laughed. 'Hardly a miracle, *señorita*. They require no planning, and we have been waiting for a chance to annihilate Rodriguez and his men for a long time. Vitas has been working with us, using himself as bait. When we realised Rodriguez was holding your brother, we knew the chance we needed had come at last. But our plans had to change when we found that you had gone down to the mission.'

'Plans?' Rachel said quietly.

'Why, yes, *señorita*.' He glanced at Vitas in surprise. 'At least——' he laughed awkwardly.

'It's all right,' she assured him levelly. 'I know what happened. You've been here for quite some time, haven't you, keeping an eye on the mission—at least two days?'

He nodded. He looked hotly aware that he had blundered in some way, but had no idea where his transgression lay. '*Si, señorita*.'

She gave him a dazzling smile, in spite of her coating of

dirt. 'You're very good at your job, *señor* captain. I hadn't the least idea there was a soldier within a hundred miles. If I had—if I'd realised the whole thing from beginning to end was a set-up, just to trap Rodriguez—then all sorts of things might have been different.'

Captain Lopez gave her an unhappy look. He said, 'You must not minimise the danger, *señorita*. Things could have gone wrong at any minute. Rodriguez is an animal, he obeys his instincts. He does not reason. He might well have shot Señor de Mendoza when he walked into the courtyard last night.'

She said sweetly, 'Oh, but the Señor is a gambler, as you must know. He would know how to calculate the odds. And when he holds a winning hand,' she added, her voice shaking with temper.

Captain Lopez gave her a baffled but respectful glance. 'You will excuse me, *señorita*? And you, Vitas? I have much to attend to.'

'Yes, go, Pablo.' There was a note of grim resignation in Vitas' voice. 'I will talk with you later, *amigo*.'

He waited until the captain was out of earshot, then said gently, 'Raquel, I know what you must be thinking.'

'Too damned right, you know!' She faced him stormily, her breasts heaving. 'I'm thinking of the fool I made of myself last night. I'm dying with shame when I think of it. You could have told me that Lopez and his men were all around, but you didn't.'

'No, I did not. But I had a reason. I had to convince Rodriguez that my surrender to him was genuine. If I'd told you the truth, your relief might have betrayed us all. One word, one gesture might have been enough.'

'Well, that's all right, then,' she said tightly. 'Because the only person I betrayed was myself. Pushing my way into your room, arguing with you, forcing myself on you— because I thought it was the last night—the only night ...' She broke off with a little gasp as his hands gripped her shoulders.

'And because you now discover you were wrong, that makes a difference?' he grated. 'Is this some strange quirk in the English character, that you are permitted to enjoy your men only in retrospect, never in the flesh? Are you trying to tell me you'd prefer me as a dead hero instead of a live lover? That was not your reaction just now when I found you weeping on top of the cliff. Or were you demonstrating your skill as an actress?'

'I'd had a terrible shock,' she flung back defiantly. 'And if we're talking about acting ability—you should be in the profession yourself, señor. Oh, before I forget,' she bent, thrusting her fingers down inside her boot. 'There's this little bit of scene dressing—that touching letter I was supposed to carry to your mother. Let's get rid of that, shall we?' She tore the letter savagely into fragments and scattered them.

'Just a minute.' He caught her arm. 'If Rodriguez' bullet had hit me just now, you would have been delivering that letter, Raquel. Do you realise that?'

'I'm only sorry it didn't!' The thought of the previous night, the things she had said, the things she had done, was burning her up inside, making her careless how she wounded him. 'But you knew it wouldn't. You weigh up every risk before you take it, don't you, señor? And all the possibilities. That's what I can't forgive. The way you faced me and gave me every reason why I shouldn't—sleep with you, except the true one. You let me sacrifice myself ...'

'Sacrifice!' He uttered a mirthless laugh. 'Dios, the virgin martyr! Besides,' he added sardonically, 'I'm sure a sacrificial victim wouldn't enter quite so fully into the spirit of the occasion. I have scratches on my back from your nails, little wildcat.'

'You dare,' she hissed, 'to insult me by reminding me of any of the humiliating details and I'll ...' She paused, lost for a suitable revenge.

'Bite?' he supplied, his brows lifting mockingly. 'You did that too, querida. Shall I strip and show you exactly where?'

She cried out and her hand came up, striking him across the face. For a moment he looked incredulous, then incredulity hardened to fury, and she did not need to look round to know that her action had been witnessed by some of Captain Lopez' men. But even so she was not prepared for what happened next.

As she turned to walk away, going in search of Mark, his hand caught her, jerking her backwards, lifting her off her feet and downwards over his bent knee. His hand descended with stinging effect four times before he released her, kicking and struggling, her cheeks flying scarlet banners of temper.

'You swine,' she choked. 'You—you . . .'

'Strike me again, Raquel, and you now know what to expect,' he said coolly.

'Don't worry,' she said between gritted teeth. 'I wouldn't lay a finger on you. I hope I never have to see you again!'

'A hope sadly destined to be unfulfilled,' he drawled.

There was something in his voice which halted her once more in her tracks.

'What do you mean?'

He shrugged. 'We had a bargain, *querida*, which I intend you to keep. I brought you here in return for—certain favours. The taste I had last night has whetted my appetite for more. This is only the beginning, Raquel.'

And it was he who walked away, leaving her staring after him white-faced and suddenly speechless.

CHAPTER TEN

CAPTAIN LOPEZ' quarters at the army post might be Spartan in their simplicity, but they boasted a small private bathroom where water gushed from taps. It also had a door that bolted, and Rachel gave a sigh of relief as she slid the bolt into place.

She had to be alone, to think, to plan what she was going to do next, and she wanted peace and privacy for this. Even Vitas, she thought, would hesitate to kick down a bathroom door which did not belong to him.

They had travelled to the post by jeep, and the presence of the driver, not to mention Pablo Lopez, had obviated conversation of a personal nature, and Rachel could only be thankful.

She winced as she lowered her body into the warm water, and each separate scratch and graze made its presence felt. Not to mention the bruises she had suffered subsequently, she thought morosely.

But if the truth were told, the slaps Vitas had administered had hurt little but her pride. The real shock had come when he had made it clear that she was not going to be allowed simply to walk out of his life.

Rachel sighed, as she gingerly soaped her shoulders and arms. Fairly or unfairly, she still felt that she had been tricked into his bed, although she supposed she should have expected little else. He had always made it plain that he would expect her to belong to him once they reached Diablo, nor had he specified the circumstances under which their agreement would be fulfilled. On the other hand, she had been equally if not more determined to keep out of his clutches. And for very good reason, as she now knew to her cost. As she had feared, she now not only belonged to him physically, but mentally and emotionally too. Even while she had been seething with temper at his duplicity, she had been totally aware of him as well.

She lifted one slim leg and began to rub the dirt from its tender surface with her fingertips.

At least the events of the last few days now presented a recognisable pattern, she thought. For instance, she knew that Vitas had been with the army during the day he had left her alone at Maria's, and that it was then he had learned for the first time not only that Mark was actually at Diablo, but that Rodriguez was there too, and that Mark was in his clutches. Lopez had been on the point of blasting his way into the mission, but Vitas had asked him to hold his hand in order to protect Mark, who might easily have been killed in a shoot-out between the army and the bandits, and for that Rachel had to be grateful at least.

It was then that Vitas had conceived the plan of going

alone to the mission to barter for the life of the young
Inglés—the brother of his *enamorador*, as Carlos would
testify. He had known quite well, of course, the price Rodriguez would demand, and his aim had been to entice the
bandit out of the mission into the open away from Mark
and towards the waiting guns of the army. But when
Rachel had unwittingly gone down to the mission herself,
then the plan had to submit to a radical last-minute change,
and it was then Vitas had decided to actually reveal the
whereabouts of the Diablo emeralds and, if possible, destroy them for ever by burying them along with Rodriguez
in a rock fall which he intended to induce by one means or
another.

Rachel paused in her task and reflected for a moment.
Now that her anger had cooled, she supposed that his attitude to her the previous night had been not quite as hypo-
critical as she thought. Perhaps he had been quite genuine
in his uncertainties. Risks were no less risky for being calculated, she thought. All sorts of things could have gone
wrong, not the least having his skull cracked open by a
lump of rock—the fate that had befallen Rodriguez.

And there was another point she had not considered.
When Vitas had walked into the circle of firelight to offer
Rodriguez his dangerous bargain, he had done so believing
that Mark was her lover. It was a sobering thought—perhaps revealing that his actions towards her were not always
guided by selfish motives, she argued. Yet that wasn't
wholly true either, because the real motivating force was
his desire, understandable enough, to have his revenge on
Rodriguez. The fact that she and Mark had become involved was really only incidental.

Mark, of course, was another problem. She had relied on
being able to leave for England almost immediately in his
company, but the army doctor who had set his leg had
vetoed any such idea. The shock of his capture by Rodriguez and his subsequent ill-treatment had all had their
effect, and bed-rest was prescribed. And to her shock Rachel
had heard Vitas calmly telling Captain Lopez that he was
ordering a private ambulance to take Mark to his house near

Villavicencio, where a nurse would be waiting to cater to his every need.

While she, no doubt, catered for the needs of the master of the house, she thought smoulderingly. And she crushed the small treacherous thought, deep inside her, which murmured that that was not nearly so distasteful a task as she might want to believe. She even surprised the beginnings of a small reminiscent smile curving the corners of her mouth, and subdued it instantly.

She had held back from giving herself to Vitas, because she had known that any such action would mean eventual heartbreak for her when he grew tired of her. She had gone to him out of love, and now she was lost forever.

She got out of the bath and began to dry herself, winding the towel sarong-style round her slim body before she opened the bathroom door. The clothes which Maria had washed for her were lying across Captain Lopez' bed. She supposed the gallant Captain who had put his quarters unreservedly at her disposal would also have loaned her a bathrobe, if she had asked. The unspoken implication behind everything he said and did was that nothing was too good for the lady whom Vitas de Mendoza chose to honour with his attentions.

She walked listlessly into the bedroom, and started violently as a hand gripped her bare arm.

'A word with you, *chica*.'

'You!' she exploded. 'Get out of here!'

'Not so loud,' he said coolly. 'I have no wish to cause a scandal.'

'You do surprise me,' she said, mustering all the sarcasm she was capable of. 'If I fight you, that's a scandal. If I sleep with you, everyone will discreetly look the other way. I like a man to have standards—even if they're double ones.'

He sighed impatiently. 'Will you stop trying to insult me, and listen to what I have to say. I haven't much time. Pablo informs me that you have been asking if he can supply you with transport to Bogota.'

'That's correct.' It was useless to deny it, but she would liked to have wrung Pablo Lopez' neck.

'I have told him that will be unnecessary. That you are coming with me to Villavicencio—to my home there.'

'Oh, no, I'm not!'

'You will do as I say, Raquel.' His tone was cold, the *gran señor* to his fingertips, she thought inconsequentially.

'You don't understand,' she said rapidly. 'I have to get back to England, to see my grandfather and tell him that Mark's alive.'

'I have already put arrangements in hand for your grandfather to be told that you are both safe and well,' he said. 'Also that you are both too shocked by your ordeal to be able to travel, and are therefore spending a period of recuperation at my home on the Llanos as the guests of my mother.'

'You take a lot for granted!' she exclaimed, biting her lip. 'And precisely how do you propose to introduce me to your mother? I wouldn't have thought she was accustomed to entertaining your mistresses. Or do you intend to introduce Mark only, and smuggle me in the back way?'

'No, I do not.' He sounded as if his hold on his temper was precarious in the extreme. 'Nor shall I introduce you as my mistress. I shall say "Madrecita, this is Raquel who is the soul of my life. Guard her and love her as if she were your own child."'

Rachel was stunned, beyond speech for a minute. Then she looked up at him wonderingly.

'I don't understand.'

'No? It is quite simple,' he said. 'You go to Villavicencio as my future wife, my *novia*.'

It was fortunate that the edge of the bed was so near, because her legs suddenly seemed unable to support her and she sank down on to it.

'You must be mad!' She was surprised that her voice sounded so steady. 'Can you give me one good reason why I should marry you?'

'I can give you several, but one will suffice.' He spoke without emotion, as if they were discussing the weather, she thought hysterically. 'The possibility we discussed last night.'

'You mean that we might have—that I might be ...' She felt the colour invade her face. 'But wouldn't it be more sensible to wait and see if it's true first?'

'No, it would not,' he said with a touch of ice. 'We will be married, and as soon as possible. My child will be born in wedlock and without a breath of scandal attaching to his name.'

'Another of your calculated risks?' she asked bitterly.

'If you choose to regard it so.'

'But Vitas,' she tried to sound reasonable, 'be honest. It —it's hardly likely, is it? After one night ...'

He gave her an incredulous look. 'Surely they don't teach you in England that it can't happen the first time with a man?'

'No, of course not.'

'I'm relieved to hear it,' he said cynically. 'At least two of my friends have found themselves with morning-sick brides before the honeymoon was over. Besides ...' he paused.

'Besides what?' she probed, in spite of herself.

'It doesn't matter.' His tone was coolly dismissive. 'Pablo requests that we dine with him.'

'I should be delighted.' Her own voice was equally distant. 'I only hope he doesn't expect me to dress for the occasion.'

For the first time a smile touched the grim contours of his mouth.

'I imagine he would expect you to wear slightly more than a towel,' he drawled. 'But he understands that skirts are not an essential part of the luggage for a horseback journey to Diablo.'

'This trip has cost me a fortune in clothes,' she said without thinking. 'Everything I wore today has had it, not to mention the stuff Carlos tore.'

'Then it is fortunate that you will be marrying a man who can afford to replenish your wardrobe for you.' His voice was dry.

Rachel stared at him, her eyes bright with dismay. She wanted to protest that the remark had been totally casual — that she hadn't even given the fact that he was wealthy a second thought. But she knew it would sound as if she was simply making excuses, and that it would be more dignified to remain silent.

Instead she found herself saying, 'You seem very sure that I will marry you.'

'Is there any real doubt?'

'I suppose not,' she admitted with a tiny sigh. 'You—always get what you want, don't you, Vitas?'

Her question seemed to hang in the odd little silence which followed.

Then he said softly, 'Do I, *chica*? At times, I wonder.'

He went out, closing the door behind him, leaving her staring blankly after him. That, she thought, must qualify as one of the strangest proposals of marriage any girl had received. In fact, he hadn't really proposed, just told her what was going to happen as if she had no say in the matter. Her hand crept to her cheek. He hadn't even said that he *wanted* to marry her, she thought, or greeted her rather stunned acceptance of his plan with any kind of pleasure. He hadn't even kissed her, and her realisation filled her with a strange desolation.

With a little shiver she reached out for her clothes, telling herself that it was only the fact that she was clad in nothing but a damp towel which was making her feel chilled to the very bone.

Rachel was not sorry to leave the army post the following day. The dinner had proved to be something of an ordeal, with some of the younger officers present exchanging furtive looks and smiles as she entered. The muttered name 'Arnaldez' from one of them soon provided her with an explanation for the air of rather knowing familiarity with which they greeted her. Carlos was presumably in the guardroom, entertaining everyone with his version of her relationship with Vitas.

But their attitude soon changed to one of somewhat

dazed respect when Vitas announced their forthcoming marriage and Pablo Lopez rose to propose their healths.

It disturbed Rachel to be given this evidence of how much female chastity was prized, and how a woman who departed from the code ordained for her might be treated. She didn't know whether to feel grateful or resentful over the difference that Vitas' announcement had made to them, although she suspected that her treatment at the post might have been very different if she had not been about to become Señora de Mendoza.

Vitas had accepted the good wishes which had been offered with courtesy, but his manner to Rachel was still distant, and she thought unhappily that she was being punished for the harsh things she had said to him at Diablo.

But if his manner at the dinner was cool, it became positively icy when he discovered that she had decided to travel to his home in the ambulance with Mark, rather than fly ahead with him in the waiting helicopter.

For a moment she thought he was going to argue with her, even order her to travel with him, but instead he turned away, telling her expressionlessly that she must act as she thought best.

As it was, the journey turned out to be a disaster. Mark was in some pain, and a thoroughly pettish mood, and he grumbled continuously, apparently blaming Vitas exclusively for the fact that he had broken his leg, and ignoring the fact that he could easily have been killed.

Rachel's patience ran out long before the journey was over, and she told him roundly that he should think himself lucky.

'I can't see how you make that out,' Mark said crossly. 'Dragging us into his feuds. Didn't he realise how dangerous it was?'

'He hardly had to drag you into anything,' Rachel pointed out. 'You were there in the thick of it, thanks to your stupid quarrel with Grandfather—and your greed.'

Mark looked sulky. 'To think that hoard of emeralds was there all the time, and I never knew,' he muttered.

'You and a million others,' she said. 'I'm glad Vitas did what he did. They're buried for ever now, and no one will ever be tempted.'

'Well, I think he's mad,' Mark said rebelliously. 'No one destroys a fortune like that.'

'Those jewels carried the seeds of their own destruction with them,' she protested. 'They were unlucky. Didn't Miguel Arviles tell you that ...'

'Miguel's an old woman,' Mark complained. 'I wouldn't have minded risking a bit of bad luck to get my hands on a few of those stones. You're not going to tell me that the high and mighty Mendoza family haven't been quietly milking them over the centuries.'

'I'm not going to tell you anything.' Rachel's tone was weary. 'You probably wouldn't believe me if I did. And I think you've had all the bad luck you can take,' she added, giving his cumbersome plaster a significant look.

Mark relapsed into a sullen silence, and Rachel found she was regretting the impulse which had decided her to travel with him. He obviously had no need of her company.

In spite of the stuffy atmosphere in the ambulance, and the persistent jolting, she managed to doze off, and woke to find that they were slowing down. She roused herself, smoothing back her dishevelled hair and running her palms, slightly damp with apprehension, down her denim-clad thighs.

The first person she saw as she descended from the ambulance was Vitas, a stranger in a lightweight formal suit. He stepped forward, and put his lips briefly on her cheek.

'Welcome to your home, Raquel,' he said quietly. 'My mother is waiting to greet you.'

She took the arm he extended to her and feeling rather foolish walked towards the arched front door and the line of waiting servants. She wished she could have made her first entrance in something a little more impressive than jeans and a shirt. Something in wild silk, she thought wistfully, and perhaps even a picture hat.

The fleeting glimpse she had been vouchsafed of the

exterior of the house had pleased her. Built in two storeys,
it seemed to reflect the elegance of a bygone era. The red
tiles of the roof had a mellow glow in the late afternoon
sun, and archways gave brief views of courtyards with
flowers and fountains, and a vivid splash of turquoise which
might have been a swimming pool.

Inside, the elegance continued, with exquisitely tiled
floors and a gracious staircase with a wrought iron balus-
trade curving up to the upper storey.

'My mother has her own suite on the first floor,' Vitas
said abruptly. 'I have ordered that your brother be taken
straight to his room. It has been a long and tiring journey
for him.'

And for me, Rachel thought, but knew if she uttered
the thought he would probably say it was her own fault and
that she could have travelled in comfort with him, instead
of riding, cramped and jolted over endless miles of dusty
roads.

She accompanied him up the stairs and along a wide
gallery to an impressive pair of carved doors at its end. He
lifted his hand to tap at one of them and glanced down
into her tense face.

'Relax, Raquel,' he advised. 'My mother will be delighted
with you. You are the answer to her prayers.'

The woman who rose to meet them as they entered was
of medium height, but her dignity and presence made her
seem taller. She wore a plain black dress in impeccable
taste and a sunburst brooch blazed on her shoulder. Rachel
found herself gathered into a scented embrace and held
warmly.

'Bless you, my child!' There were tears in the Señora's
eyes as she stood back. 'And bless you, Vitas, for bringing her to me. She is as lovely as an angel. What an exquisite bride she will make, and how happy I shall be to dress
her. It is so long since Juanita was married.'

'At least two years,' he supplied drily. 'If you wish to
talk to Raquel about clothes, then I will leave you and
make sure that her brother is comfortable and has all that
he needs.'

Rachel felt unutterably self-conscious as the doors closed behind him, and she was left alone with the Señora.

'Come and sit down, my child.' The Señora waved her towards a sofa set in front of the wide window. 'I shall not detain you long. You will wish to go to your room and bathe and rest before dinner. Vitas is having your luggage sent here from Asuncion, but I have chosen a few things that were Juanita's for you to use in the meantime. If you decide on a dress for this evening, my maid will carry out any small alterations that are necessary.' She smiled at Rachel. 'Later of course you will choose your own maid, but at first several girls from the estate will wait on you in turn so that you can get to know them and decide which will suit you best.'

She picked up a piece of embroidery and began to work on it.

'I have also arranged for my dressmaker to come here the day after tomorrow, when you are rested, with patterns and samples of material for your wedding dress.'

Rachel swallowed. 'So soon?'

The Señora's eyes rested on her with a faintly quizzical expression. She said gently, 'Dear child, from what my impetuous son has told me, it seems to me that your marriage should take place without delay.'

Rachel felt herself blush to the roots of her hair, the few remaining shreds of her poise scattered.

'He has told you everything?' she asked in a low voice.

'He has always told me everything.' The Señora paused in her stitching. 'This has distressed you? Do you perhaps expect me to be shocked—to hold you in contempt because you gave yourself outside the sacrament? Surely you cannot think so. That night you spent with my son might well have been his last on earth. Do you think I could despise the girl who held back the darkness for him?'

Rachel felt tears prick at her eyelids. She said, 'I—I didn't know what to expect.' After Mark's hostility, she supposed she had anticipated the worst.

'You are tired,' the Señora said soothingly. 'And you have suffered a terrible ordeal at the hands of that evil one,

Rodriguez.' She crossed herself. 'May God have mercy upon his soul. I will ring and have Josita take you to your room.'

Josita turned out to be an elderly woman with a gaunt face, but when she smiled she was transformed, and she smiled a great deal as she watched Rachel take her first awed look round the bedroom she had been taken to.

The bed itself was enchantment enough—four carved posts and a mass of crisp white frills cascading down to the carpet. The sunlight coming into the room was diffused through the palest of silk drapes, and each window was flanked by floor-length curtains in heavy brocade, looped back by matching cords. The carpet and walls complemented each other in pale orchid pink.

After Maria's attentions, Rachel submitted resignedly to being helped out of her jeans and shirt and wrapped in a swansdown-trimmed peignoir while Josita showed her the dresses the Señora had mentioned. It was obvious the maid favoured the first one she displayed for Rachel, a classic white chiffon, with billowing diaphanous sleeves, and she was disappointed when Rachel shook her head, biting her lip slightly. Under the circumstances, she thought wryly, there was no way in which she was going to present herself downstairs clad in virginal white under Vitas' cynical gaze.

Eventually she chose a dark blue model covered in small white polka dots, essentially Spanish in design, with an off-the-shoulder bodice and wide flounced skirt. The length was right, but her waist was more slender than that of the absent Juanita, and Josita bore the dress away to make the necessary adjustments.

Rachel lay on the bed and tried to relax. The Señora's welcome had done much to warm the coldness deep inside her, but she knew that it was the reassurance of Vitas' arms around her that she really needed.

His coolness frightened her. Even his mockery would be preferable, she thought, or the passion she had tried to escape. Had her bitter rejection of him after they had escaped from the tunnel at Diablo changed him so much?

she wondered. Thoughts went spinning through her mind in hazy confusion.

The Señora was right, she told herself sleepily. I am tired. In fact I'm exhausted. And it will all seem very different tomorrow.

But it was no different the following day, or the day after that, or any of the weeks which followed.

Rachel felt as if she was living in a dream. She stood like an automaton while a small dark woman pinned and tacked, prodded and pulled at her, endless yards of cream silk chiffon spilling around her. She walked in the gardens beside the fountain. She visited Mark while he was confined to his room on doctor's orders. She talked with the Señora. She swam in the swimming pool wearing a bikini of Juanita's, which Josita also adapted for her. She sunbathed. She changed for dinner and descended the staircase to the *salón* where the Señora and the ever-growing number of relations summoned to attend Vitas' wedding waited. After dinner, she sat and made stilted conversation designed to improve her Spanish, trying not to let her eyes stray too often to the other side of the room where Vitas sat. And when the small tinkling clock on the side table sounded the hour of ten, she would rise, receive the Señora's goodnight kiss and walk to the door where Vitas waited to kiss her hand and then her cheek coolly and swiftly.

The first time it happened, she almost hadn't believed it. She had walked up to her room in a daze, and let the round-faced girl waiting nervously there help her undress and put on a delicate lace nightgown. Then she had lain there in the darkness staring across the room at the closed door, waiting almost painfully for it to open and for him to come to her.

She had no doubt that he would come. He had warned her at Diablo that her debt to him was by no means paid. But there was more to it than that. She wanted him to come. She lay, watching the darkness and wishing him beside her. Even when the entire house was quiet, she still waited for him to come to her.

But her bedroom door remained closed, not just for that night, but for each night that followed. He never came near her. In the daytime—on the rare occasions when she saw him—he was charming to her in an aloof way, as she guessed he would be to any woman guest under his roof. She saw him exercise the same charm on a bevy of wide-eyed young cousins and a dragon of an aunt from Magdalena.

But for much of the time, he was absent. The Señora explained that he was much occupied with business.

'He works twice as hard now,' she said smilingly, 'so that after his marriage he can devote his time to his lovely young bride.'

The lovely young bride returned the smile with an effort and wondered bleakly whether she featured in his future plans at all.

Yet she could not deny that he was thoughtful. He had arranged for a diplomat friend based in London to call on Sir Giles, and the reassuring news had been sent back that her grandfather, though anxious, was continuing to make excellent progress. Her luggage had been brought from Asuncion, and her wardrobe added to during two delightful shopping trips to Bogota with the Señora.

In many ways her days could not have been more completely filled, yet they were empty. And when she realised that in just over a week she would stand in the family chapel and be married to a man who was becoming more of a stranger with every minute that passed, a cry of silent panic rose within her.

And there was no one she could turn to, not even Mark, who had made a rapid recovery and was now mobile again with the help of a crutch. He had become friendly with one of Vitas' male cousins, a young man of his own age but double the sophistication called Jaime who shared Mark's passion for fast cars, and was quite content to drive him into Villavicencio or around the dirt roads of the vast estate.

Rachel had gone with them once, but she had not enjoyed

the trip because Jaime's style of driving did not impress her. But she thought she could learn to love the rolling grasslands that stretched for miles as far as the eye could see, if she could be shown them by her lover. But Vitas had not offered to show her the ranch, and she was determined not to ask him. She had discovered through talking to Jaime and the others that he not only bred cattle, but had vast industrial interests too, which he had never mentioned. Rachel thought with a pang that the more she found out about him, the less she seemed to know, and yet soon she would belong to him in the most intimate relationship of all.

It couldn't go on like this, she told herself. She couldn't marry him, expecting to be excluded from everything that was meaningful in his life. He couldn't really expect her to turn into a docile Colombian wife, without a thought in her head except the latest fashion and how to prevent her husband's eyes from straying . . .

This was the thought which plagued her the most, she admitted miserably to herself. Every time she remembered the photograph she had seen at Maria's, pain slashed at her like a knife. She could be looking at herself, she thought, hungry, pleading for a warmth, a love that would ever be denied her.

She wanted to be alone with him, she thought. She wanted to go to him and tell him all her doubts, her uncertainties, and feel his arms close around her. He still wanted her, she thought bleakly, or so he had led her to believe. Perhaps that was not even true any more. But one way or another, she needed to find out before they took an irrevocable step that could ruin both their lives.

She chose a morning when she knew he would be in the estate office at the back of the house. The door to the office was open, and she saw with a lift of her heart that he was alone, packing papers into a briefcase, his dark face absorbed and rather remote as he bent over the massive heavily carved desk which dominated the room.

He did not see her at first, and she was forced to clear her throat to attract his attention. His head came up immediately and she saw his brows lift with surprise.

'An unexpected honour, *querida*,' he drawled. 'Was there something you wanted?'

Rachel was tempted to say baldly, 'Yes—you.' But he was too much of a stranger these days for that. She came forward slowly, her eyes fixed on his face. In spite of his constrained manner to her and the formal suits he wore these days, the eye-patch gave him an undeniably rakish air.

'I wanted to talk,' she said. 'I—I seem to see so little of you these days.'

He glanced at his watch. 'Unfortunately I have to leave for a business appointment almost immediately. But I am flattered—and surprised that you should seek me out. It was not long ago you told me you never wanted to set eyes on me again.'

She moved her shoulders defensively. 'Well, that was then. But we're going to be married, aren't we?' She tried to smile. 'I can hardly avoid seeing you sometimes when you're my husband.'

He gave her an ironic look. 'How true. Is that why you've come here, Raquel? To find out exactly what demands I intend to make of you once you are my wife?'

'No,' she protested, 'it isn't that at all. I just want to talk—to get to know you,' she added in a low voice.

He fastened the catches on his briefcase. 'Again you flatter me. Yet there are those who would say that we are already more—intimately acquainted than any unmarried couple have any right to be.'

'That isn't what I mean, and you know it.' She watched him pick up the briefcase and take another swift glance at his watch. 'Don't let me detain you.'

'We'll talk tonight, if that is what you want,' he said. 'Perhaps it's time we did. But you must forgive me now.'

He walked towards the door, but as he drew level with her, he slowed almost imperceptibly, and she felt his brooding gaze rest on her face, on her parted lips. She felt herself sway towards him as if he had hypnotised her, her body yearning towards his. She wanted his mouth on hers, his hands to discover all the sweet secrets her body longed to offer him.

And then the moment was over. Vitas strode to the door, gave her a brief, unsmiling bow and was gone.

Rachel stood still in the centre of the room as if she had been transfixed. She felt rejected, outcast, totally alone. She swung round and caught the edge of the desk with her hands, pressing the sharp carving which decorated it almost convulsively into the soft flesh of her palms, welcoming the ache it brought her. At least it still proved she was alive and had feelings. She wanted to throw herself down on the floor and cry, but she knew she had to leave. The two secretaries who worked in the office must be at their coffee break, but they would be returning soon, and she had no wish to be caught by them standing alone in Vitas' office, looking as if she was about to faint. She was just walking towards the door, when one of the telephones on the desk rang imperatively. Rachel halted, looking back at it doubtfully. She wasn't sure whether the call was coming in on the house telephone or the outside line. If it was an outside call, she didn't think her Spanish would stand up to coping with any long explanations that she was not one of the secretaries. On the other hand, it might be important.

With sudden decision she went back and picked up the telephone.

It was a woman's voice that spoke, warm, and with an unmistakable American accent.

'Vitas, honey? There's been a change of plan. It will be easier if we meet at the hotel.' There was a pause as if she was waiting for a reaction, and then she said sharply, 'Vitas? Are you there?'

Rachel passed her tongue over suddenly dry lips. She said, 'I'm sorry, señora. Señor de Mendoza has already left. I'm afraid the original arrangements will have to stand.'

And she laid the receiver very gently back into its rest.

Rachel sat huddled on the back seat of Jaime's car. She still didn't know what impulse had prompted her to run through

the house and out into the sunshine, and she had found
Jaime there, helping Mark into the car. They were just
off to Villavicencio, and they were clearly amazed when
she asked if she might go with them.

'Jump in.' Mark studied her white face. 'Though you
don't really look as if you ought to be going anywhere,'
he added with brutal candour. 'And what about your hand-
bag? Don't you want . . .'

'It doesn't matter,' she interrupted. 'Can't we just go—
please!'

Mark and Jaime exchanged a long look, and she heard
Jaime murmur something about bridal nerves. Let them
think what they wanted, she told herself. It didn't matter.
Nothing mattered.

All the way into Villavicencio, she sat silent in the back
of the car, indifferent even to the speed at which they were
travelling, her eyes unseeing as she gazed out at the splen-
dours of the countryside. Someone had told her at dinner
one night that the Llanos was splendid hunting country,
abounding in deer and wild pigs. She felt as if she knew
what the victim of such a hunt must feel as it crouched
in the long grass, waiting, its nerves screaming, for the
inevitable kill. Perhaps it welcomed the *coup de grâce* when
it came, she thought. Perhaps it was the uncertainty, the
waiting which was the real cruelty.

Maybe when she saw for her own eyes Vitas with another
woman, then her feelings would experience the numbness
of death. She hoped so, because the pain was almost more
than she could bear.

What had made her think that everything they had been
through together, the danger they had shared had meant
anything? He wanted her, and he had taken her, and now
he was prepared to marry her because there might be a
child on the way, and it was time he married and produced
an heir for the Mendoza lands and wealth. But that was
all. To him, she was just another woman, and his life would
go on in exactly the same way as before. She wondered
how many other times he had met his American mistress
under the guise of attending a business meeting.

No wonder his manner had seemed so strained when she confronted him in the office! Perhaps his conscience was troubling him at last. He had said it was time they talked. Perhaps he was going to tell her all about it, to make it clear that their marriage was to be on his terms and that as his wife she would be expected to look the other way and not demand a fidelity he was incapable of showing her.

Jaime was puzzled when she began asking him about hotels in Villavicencio, but he gave the information she wanted. There were several, he told her, but the Hotel Popayan was the most favoured by tourists—and the most expensive.

Mark said with a touch of irritation, 'You don't need a hotel, love. Jaime and I will take you to lunch. There's a place that he says does the best *tamales* in the Llanos.'

'Perhaps I'll meet you there later,' she said. 'But I—I have some things to do first.'

'Not more shopping!' Mark groaned. 'I'm glad it's Vitas who has to pay for all this, that's all.'

'This time,' she said, 'he doesn't have to pay for a thing.'

Inside the foyer of the Popayan, it was all air-conditioned luxury. There was a sprinkling of people occupying the chairs round the small tables, and Rachel found herself an empty table shaded by a massive display of tropical plants. Their perfume made her feel dizzy and a little sick.

And also a little mad. After all, she didn't even know whether this was the right hotel. Perhaps there were other establishments which rented rooms by the hour to illicit lovers. And she couldn't ask at the desk if Vitas was in the hotel, or for the number of the suite he was visiting.

And then she saw him. Saw them. They were coming down the stairs, and he was holding her arm, gently and protectively. It was the woman in the photograph, Rachel saw, but she looked very different. She was smiling for one thing, her face happy and relaxed, and there was an air of luxurious fulfilment about her which nothing could disguise. Just as the elegant maternity outfit she was wearing did nothing to disguise the fact that she was very pregnant.

Rachel shrank into her chair. It was all so much worse than she had ever expected—ever dreamed. She thought for one horrified moment that they were going to come and sit at one of the tables. That he would look up and see her sitting there, watching them.

But she was spared that at least. But nothing else. The woman spoke quite clearly, seeing no reason, obviously, to lower her voice or hide her feelings.

'Vitas, I'm so happy. Happier than I ever dreamed possible. But can it last?'

And his reply. No mockery in his voice, just affection.

'It can last just as long as you wish, Virginia, _querida_. Always remember that. It is in your hands.'

Rachel watched them walk to the door of the hotel. They paused there, and this time they were too far away for her to hear what was being said. But eventually the woman ·Virginia laughed, and Vitas, also smiling, lifted her hand to his lips. Then he walked out into the sunshine of the street. The woman came back alone, humming a little tune as she walked past the table where Rachel sat. For a moment their eyes met, those of Virginia incurious, and full of a strange serenity. Then Rachel tore her gaze away, and leaned forward to pour some more of the coffee she did not want and was incapable of swallowing into her cup.

Rachel closed her suitcase and took one last look round the room. She had left nothing that belonged to her, but had taken nothing else. All the clothes that had once belonged to Juanita, who was arriving tomorrow with her husband to attend the wedding, and whom she would now never meet, were hanging in the wardrobe along with items from the expensive, luxurious trousseau that Señora de Mendoza was delighting in lavishing upon her.

There was only one last thing. She unclasped the medallion Vitas had given her from around her neck and put it down on the table beside the bed where it couldn't be missed. She had left no note, no explanation. Perhaps she should have done, but she did not know where to begin. It was better this way, she told herself, to simply remove herself from his life. There was no way she could stay and face further heartbreak.

All the way back from Villavicencio while Jaime and Mark talked in the front, she had made her plans. She knew the car journey from Villavicencio to Bogota took roughly three hours, and she knew too that Jaime rarely removed his keys from the ignition, and usually left his car standing at the side of the house. All she had to do was wait until the household was asleep, then creep downstairs, let herself out of the house—and borrow it. She would leave it at a garage in Bogota, she thought, and ask them to notify Jaime that it was there.

The thought of returning to England to face Grandfather and the inevitable questions was not an appealing one, but she had no other choice. Nor could she take Mark into her confidence. He would probably tell her she had only herself to blame for getting mixed up with a man like Vitas de Mendoza in the first place. And she supposed he had a fair point.

She had to try and make herself think like that, try to whip her anger, her hurt into a blaze against him because that was her only salvation. She could not, would not become his wife knowing that she would be expected to turn a blind eye to his affairs.

There was no doubt in her mind that his relationship with Virginia was now firmly established, and would not be lightly jettisoned. And there was the coming baby to think of. Rachel swallowed painfully. At least she now knew for a fact that she did not have a similar problem. She didn't carry Vitas' child within her, but another woman did. She wondered if Virginia had left her husband. Perhaps she was waiting for a divorce, and with herself out of the way, she and Vitas would then get married.

She smothered the little sob which rose involuntarily in her throat. She had to make herself see that she was having a lucky escape. What hope could there ever have been for Vitas and herself, even if she had not found out about Virginia? They came from two very different worlds, apart from anything else. He'd seen her and fancied her, but there was nothing in that on which to build the sort of permanent, caring relationship she wanted. But she'd allowed the thought that he'd asked her to marry him, that he wanted to keep her with him to blind her to all of this. She'd almost believed that her own love, her own caring would be a kind of alchemy to turn her dark pirate, her millionaire playboy from a casual lover into a loving husband.

Well, the more fool she. She opened her bedroom door cautiously and peeped out. There was not a sound to be heard. She had not gone down to dinner, mendaciously pleading a headache, because Vitas had told her that they would talk, and she knew she would not be able to bear a confrontation with him. She had asked not to be disturbed and her wish had been respected.

She wished, as she tiptoed along the gallery to the stairs, that she had at least been able to say goodbye to Señora de Mendoza.

She was trembling as she reached the foot of the stairs. She went soft-footed across the hall to the main door, and found to her surprise that it was unbolted. She turned the massive handle and quietly let herself out. She took two steps and then she heard it—the sound of a car approaching. She stood there, stranded. She couldn't run with her case, but she couldn't simply drop it and hide because the newcomer would be bound to see it. She looked round wildly as powerful headlights stabbed the gloom, and the car swung in under the archway and came to rest only a few yards from where she stood, still clutching her suitcase, her eyes dilating in terror, because she knew quite suddenly and without the slightest doubt just who was driving that car.

He climbed unhurriedly out of the driving seat and walked to where she was standing.

'And where do you think you are going?' His voice sounded molten with anger.

'I don't think,' she retorted. 'I know—and it's back to England.'

'May I ask why?'

She shrugged. 'I had a letter this morning from my agent,' she said. 'I've had a marvellous offer of a new play—the sort of chance you can't afford to turn down. So I'm taking it.'

'And your prior commitment—to me?'

She said, 'I don't think you really wanted me to hold you to it. I mean, there's no need now. I suppose I should have told you really, set your mind at rest. There isn't going to be a baby, so you don't have to worry about me any more.'

'Not worry about you,' he repeated softly. 'Of all the harsh things you have said to me, *querida*, I think this is the cruellest.'

'Don't mention cruelty to me!' she cried.

'And what is that supposed to mean?'

'It doesn't matter,' she muttered wretchedly. 'Nothing matters. Please let me go.'

Vitas swore under his breath and bending forward he snatched her case from her hand and flung it away into the darkness.

'You are going nowhere,' he said. 'Without me, you go nowhere—do you hear me, Raquel?'

He picked her up into his arms and carried her back into the house, into the *salón* where he dumped her unceremoniously on one of the sofas.

She said, 'You can't treat me like this. I'm a free agent. I ...'

'You are going to be my wife,' he said.

'No,' she shook her head. 'You—you heard what I told you, Vitas. There's no need for that—for any more pretence. I—I'm not pregnant, so we can end this farce right here and now.'

'A farce?' he repeated incredulously. 'You describe the prospect of being my wife as a farce?'

'Yes, I do,' she cried. 'And—and I don't even have the leading role.'

'What is that supposed to mean?' he said slowly. 'You had better explain yourself, Raquel.'

'I saw you,' she said exhaustedly. 'I answered the phone in your room, just after you'd left, and it was her—your Virginia. She—she's the woman in the photograph, isn't she? The one you took into the *cordillera* with you?'

'Yes,' he said. 'What of it?'

'You're quite shameless about it!' She stared up at him.

'I have yet to hear why I am supposed to feel shame. You say you saw me. Am I to infer that you followed me to Villavicencio because of this telephone call?'

'Yes,' she said. 'And I saw you there together at the hotel. I saw—how she was. I heard what she said to you—about being happy.' She swallowed. 'Well, when I'm out of the way you can be even happier. But you can't expect me to —marry you, and then look the other way while you amuse yourself.'

His dark face looked as if it had been carved out of stone, as remote as the highest peak of the Andes and as cold.

'You think that was my intention?'

'I don't know what else to think,' she said wretchedly. 'But I've got to get away—back to England. There— there's nothing to keep me here, after all. And once I've gone you can marry your Virginia—if that's what you want.'

'How kind of you to consider my wishes, *querida*,' he drawled, and she flinched as his words seemed to flick like the tongue of a whip across her skin. 'But marriage with Virginia has little appeal for me. I imagine her husband too might have some objections.'

'Her husband?' she echoed.

'His name is Robert,' he said icily. 'I have known him— known them both for some years. He was responsible for installing some plant at one of the factories in Medellin, and we became friends as a result of this. We are negotiating about another project with the company he represents, and he came to Villavicencio for some informal talks with me before going on to Medellin to talk to my board. Today we were to meet for lunch, but Virginia wished to change the venue because Robert was suffering slightly from a migraine. She told me she had tried to contact me without success when she met me. I returned to their suite with her, but Robert was not well enough for our discussions to proceed, so I left.' He paused. 'Is there anything else you wish to know about how I spent my day?'

Rachel did not reply and after a moment he went on, 'Your eyes and busy little ears deceived you, *querida*. Virginia is not expecting my child, but Robert's. A child they have both longed for since their marriage. And *si*, she did speak of her happiness, because she has not always been happy. A year ago, perhaps more, she knew Robert was— involved with someone else. In some ways she blamed herself for this. Because there was no child, she had thrown herself into her career—had allowed other things to assume too much importance. When she found out about the other woman, she was bitter and unhappy.'

'So she turned to you,' Rachel said in a low voice.

'*Si*, she turned to me,' he said ironically. 'But not in the way you imagine. She needed to get away both from Robert and the situation which was causing her so much pain. She wanted to see things clearly, to decide what she wanted from her life. I took her with me into the *cordillera* to give her time to think. But I did not make love to her, then or ever. She needed a friend, and I was a friend to her.'

Rachel looked down at her tightly clasped hands. She said, 'But she wanted you. I saw that photograph. I saw how she looked at you.'

'She thought she wanted me. She was lonely and unhappy, and she thought Robert didn't care any more,' He sat down on the sofa beside her, lifting her chin in his hand, forcing her to look at him. There were taut bitter lines round his mouth. 'You have always had a low opinion of me, haven't you, *querida*? Do you really think I added to Virginia's problems by sleeping with her?'

No, she didn't, but somehow it was impossible to tell him so because that might lead in turn to other confessions she would prefer not to make. It was better for him to think she had a low opinion of him than to know that she had leapt to conclusions because she was half sick with jealousy and despair. From the very first, the thought of Virginia in his arms had been a nightmare to her, although she hadn't realised why.

She said stiffly, 'I'm sorry—I assumed ...'

'You assume altogether too much,' he said savagely. 'You assume that I'm marrying you because you may be *encinta*. You assume that once we are married, I cannot wait to be unfaithful to you. You assume that I am just going to let you walk out of my life. Well, you are wrong, *querida*, on all three counts. And don't lie to me about this wonderful offer you have had. All the mail that comes to this house passes first through my hands, and I know there has been no such letter. I am not quite a fool.'

'And I'm not a fool either.' There were tears in her eyes, but she didn't care. 'I—I may have been wrong about Virginia, but there have been other women. You can't deny that.'

'I wouldn't even try.' He raised his brows haughtily. 'Do you really expect me to have lived like a monk before you came into my life?'

'I don't expect anything of you,' she said wearily. 'I don't know you, can't you see that? I don't know anything about you,' she went on in a kind of panic. 'Anything!'

Except what you're like as a lover, an inner voice reminded her. Except your strength and your warmth, and the way you were gentle with me at first, and later, not gentle at all.

'How strange that you should feel that,' he said bleakly, 'when from the first moment I saw you, I felt that I had always known you. Always been waiting for you to come to me. Why did you think I came after you as I did? Because I wanted a mistress?' he laughed harshly. 'There were other willing women, so why saddle myself with someone who only wanted to fight me? I followed you because

I had to, and if Carlos had hurt you I would have killed him with my bare hands. And if you leave me, I'll go on following you—back to England, if that's how it must be.'

She stared at him, her eyes wide and fixed on his face, seeing for the first time the hurt and the uncertainty underlying the cynicism.

She said, 'Vitas ....' and the next moment she was in his arms, and he was kissing her with a passion that seemed to sweep away her doubts forever.

'*Amada*,' he whispered. '*Alma de mi vida*. Don't you know that I've been waiting for you since the beginning of time? Little one, sweet fool, I'll never let you go.'

'I didn't know.' She was between laughter and tears. 'I thought that you—just wanted to go to bed with me. You did rather give me that impression at first and ...'

He settled her in his arms, holding her against the warmth of his body, one hand cupping the delicate swell of her breast.

'Perhaps it was true at first,' he confessed. 'All I knew was that I wanted you so much I thought I would go crazy —especially when I went into your room at the hotel and saw you lying there asleep, so beautiful and so helpless.' He groaned. 'I used to lie awake at night torturing myself with the memory of how you'd looked. I knew from the first that it would be different with you, *querida*, but I didn't in honesty know that I would want to marry you.' He gave her a sardonic look. 'That came later—that first night at the *finca* when I walked into our room and saw you standing by the bed in that nightgown of Maria's.'

'You were hateful.' Shyly, she put up a hand and stroked his cheek. Vitas captured the hand and carried it to his mouth.

'I was overwhelmed,' he corrected. 'I'd sat through that interminable meal with only one thought—that at last I was going to get you into bed.' He smiled reminiscently. 'I flew across that courtyard when Maria came back as if I had wings on my feet. But when I opened the door what did I see? A bride, *mi amada*—very young, very lovely, very shy—and very virginal. I felt that if I as much as touched you—even if you gave yourself willingly—it would be a violation. I knew then that I had to have you as my wife—but before I could say anything I had to destroy Rodriguez. I had pursued him for too long to let him escape me because I had fallen in love. Besides, living, he was always a threat.' He shuddered. 'I will never forget what I felt when I realised you had gone down to the mission. I had to bank on the fact that his greed for the Diablo emeralds would outweigh any other consideration—such as the pleasure of killing you slowly in front of me.'

'The emeralds,' she said in a low voice. 'You deliberately destroyed the mine.'

'It is better destroyed,' he said flatly. 'My father died to protect its secret. I was not prepared to carry that responsibility. Too many lives had been lost over the centuries.'

'But when it was all over—when you asked me to marry you,' Rachel said slowly. 'You were so cold. You made me think it was just the possibility that I might be pregnant that mattered.'

'You seemed too angry with me to listen to the things I really wanted to say to you,' he said drily. 'And I was a little angry myself.'

'But you went on being cold,' she protested. 'I thought that after—what had happened between us—you didn't want me any more. That you were marrying me because you felt—obliged to.'

'Not want you, *mi alma*?' His mouth explored hers with a lingering possessiveness which devastated her. 'There hasn't been an hour of the day and night since you came to my house that I haven't craved for you as a man lost in a desert craves water.'

'Then why . . .' she began. He laid a caressing finger on her lips, silencing her.

'Because you were now my *novia*,' he said simply. 'My future wife. My mother forgave us that one lapse, but made it clear that the rest of our courtship would be conducted in a way that would give no scandal. I decided my only course must be to keep at a distance.'

She stole a mischievous glance at him. 'Then it's just as well that no one can see us now!'

'Just as well.' He returned her smile. 'And tomorrow I shall tell Madrecita that our wedding will take place the following day, because that is when I intend to begin our honeymoon whether we are married or not.'

'I'm afraid she'll be cross with us,' Rachel said dreamily. 'My trousseau isn't ready yet.'

He gave her a sardonic grin. 'Your clothes don't really interest me, *querida*, although the lack of them does. I'll take you to Rio for the first few days and buy you what you need there. Then we'll go on to England and visit your grandfather.'

'And afterwards?'

'Afterwards we come home.' His arms tightened around her. 'My country is very different from yours, *querida*. Will you be able to look on it as your home eventually?'

She slid her arms up round his neck, drawing him down to her. Vitas was taking her to England, though it would not be her that her grandfather would be waiting impatiently to see, she knew, but Mark. Yet that no longer had the power to hurt her.

'Home, my darling, is wherever you are,' she told him softly, and kissed him.

The Mills & Boon Rose is the Rose of Romance

Look for the Rose of Romance this Christmas

Four titles by favourite authors in a specially-produced gift pack.

THAT BOSTON MAN *by Janet Dailey*

MY SISTER'S KEEPER *by Rachel Lindsay*

ENEMY FROM THE PAST *by Lilian Peake*

DARK DOMINION *by Charlotte Lamb*

UNITED KINGDOM £2.20 net
REP. OF IRELAND £2.40

First time in paperback. Published 12th October.
You can obtain this gift pack from your local paperback retailer.

189

Titles available this month in the Mills & Boon ROMANCE Series

THE KURRANULLA ROUND *by Dorothy Cork*
Matty's uncle wanted to see her married to Dirk Reasoner,
but Matty knew something her uncle didn't — and that was
why Dirk would never trust and respect her, let alone love
her . . .

ACROSS THE GREAT DIVIDE *by Kerry Allyne*
It was Jerome whom Nicole loved — so why was it the annoy-
ing Lang Jamieson who occupied so much of her thoughts?

FLAME OF DIABLO *by Sara Craven*
Vitas de Mendoza agreed to help Rachel find her brother —
but at a price. Would she find the price too high? Or would
she pay — far too willingly?

BLUE LOTUS *by Margaret Way*
Susan was rescued from the rain forest of Queensland by
Devin Chandler and taken to recover at his cattle station — a
private kingdom where the king made his own laws . . .

FRUSTRATION *by Charlotte Lamb*
Considering the tumultuous circumstances of their first
meeting, it was hardly surprising that Jake Lang should
despise and dislike Natalie Buchan . . .

A DANGEROUS MAN *by Mary Wibberley*
When Tania met Bryden Kane she realised that he was a
dangerous man to know — certainly she could sense the
danger to her own heart.

APOLLO'S SEED *by Anne Mather*
Martha had been virtually forced to return to Greece and her
husband Dion. But it was clear that his only reason for wanting
her was to get their child back.

A MAN TO WATCH *by Jane Donnelly*
To Harriet, Jotham Gaul was nothing but an irritating boor
who told her she had nothing but her looks — but why should
she care about his opinion?

A CERTAIN SMILE *by Marjorie Lewty*
When Amanda discovered her father, she found herself
whisked into a world of wealth, of tycoons, of sophistication
— and a world that also contained Blair Craddock . . .

STORMY AFFAIR *by Margaret Mayo*
Who did Hamed Ben Slouma think he was, spoiling Amber's
peaceful holiday in Tunisia by whisking her off to his house
and announcing that he was going to marry her?

Mills & Boon Romances
— all that's pleasurable in Romantic Reading!

Available November 1979

191

Choose from this selection of

Mills & Boon
FAVOURITES
—ALL HIGHLY RECOMMENDED

ORDER NOW FOR DIRECT DELIVERY

☐ 1555
RETURN TO DEVIL'S VIEW
Rosemary Carter

☐ 1556
TOGETHER AGAIN
Flora Kidd

☐ 1557
SHADOW OF THE PAST
Robyn Donald

☐ 1558
THE TEMPESTUOUS FLAME
Carole Mortimer

☐ 1559
A ROSE FROM LUCIFER
Anne Hampson

☐ 1560
THE MAN ON THE PEAK
Katrina Britt

☐ 1561
SOLITAIRE
Sara Craven

☐ 1562
WITH THIS RING
Mary Wibberley

☐ 1563
THE JUDAS TRAP
Anne Mather

☐ 1564
SWEET COMPULSION
Victoria Woolf

☐ 1565
CHATEAU IN THE PALMS
Anne Hampson

☐ 1566
ONE MORE RIVER TO CROSS
Essie Summers

☐ 1567
SAVAGE POSSESSION
Margaret Pargeter

☐ 1568
LURE OF EAGLES
Anne Mather

☐ 1569
MIDNIGHT SUN'S MAGIC
Betty Neels

☐ 1570
LOVE IS A FRENZY
Charlotte Lamb

☐ 1571
THIS SIDE OF PARADISE
Kay Thorpe

☐ 1572
A LAND CALLED DESERET
Janet Dailey

☐ 1573
TANGLED SHADOWS
Flora Kidd

☐ 1574
THE PASSIONATE WINTER
Carole Mortimer

ONLY 55p EACH

SIMPLY TICK ☑ YOUR SELECTION(S) ABOVE, THEN JUST COMPLETE AND POST THE ORDER FORM OVERLEAF ▶